MEAD
PUBLIC LIBRARY

In memory of
Charles E. Carroll

Donated by family
and friends

2010

IF I COULD FLY

JUDITH ORTIZ COFER

If I Could Fly

FARRAR STRAUS GIROUX
NEW YORK

The quotes on bird behavior in the part titles are from *Pigeons and Doves of the World* by Derek Goodwin, 3rd ed., © Natural History Museum, London, 1970. 1983.

macteenbooks.com

Library of Congress Cataloging-in-Publication Data

Cofer, Judith Ortiz.
    If I could fly / Judith Ortiz Cofer. — 1st ed.
      p. cm.
    Summary: When fifteen-year-old Doris's mother, a professional singer, returns to Puerto Rico and her father finds a girlfriend, Doris cares for a neighbor's pigeons and relies on friends as she begins to find her own voice and wings.
    ISBN: 978-0-374-33517-5
    [1. Family problems—Fiction. 2. Separation (Psychology)—Fiction. 3. Puerto Ricans—New Jersey—Fiction. 4. Singers—Fiction. 5. Pigeons—Fiction. 6. New Jersey—Fiction.] I. Title.

PZ7.O765If 2011
[Fic]—dc22

2010022309

This book is dedicated to the best teacher I know, Mr. C.

What the Bird Believes

What the bird sees:

In the alley between two buildings
a mother cat curls around her newborn kittens
as a hungry dog approaches, following the tracks
left last night, reading smells like a newspaper,
or like phosphorescent road signs. He is set for
the chase. On the sidewalk, a girl in a bright red coat
sees the shadow of wings at her feet,
looks up, and trips over the street person sleeping
on a cardboard box. The noise scares the dog in the alley
into a run. He misses the cat nursing her kittens,
distracted by new clues to this day: a garbage can,
a bag of chicken bones, so much treasure in his path
he can't turn back for old joys. He barks up at the bird.
Called out by the dog, a woman remembers
to put the day-old loaf of bread in her bag before
she walks to the park.

What the bird wants:

The bird spots the old woman on her bench.
He flies in ever-closer circles, hovering over her head.
She is slow in her movements, eyes unfocused,
she is looking deep into her loneliness. The bird is hungry,
but he must wait until she notices his graceful dance,
created just for her out of thin air. The bird dips and rises
within her vision until the woman's eyes lift up toward the sky.
Because he is there, she notices the promise of a new day,
and she breathes the crisp air. Soon she will remember why
she is here.

What the bird gets:

The old woman will scatter her offerings before her,
and in a soft voice, as if she were praying, she will sing out,
Ven, paloma, ven. And he will alight at her feet
to eat his daily bread crumbs. The bird believes
she is here for him, and she believes
he is there for her.

Part One

In display flight a pigeon usually spreads its wings widely, beats them rather slowly through a wider arc than usual and often makes a loud clapping noise when so doing.

It [does seem] likely that those elements of the display flight which actually slow down forward movement—the wide, slower wing beats, spreading tail, gliding instead of beating the wings—originate in a conflict between tendencies to move away from and to remain in or return to a certain area.

1

When I come out of my room ready to go to church, I find Papi in the kitchen drinking yesterday's coffee. He's looking *perdido*, lost, in deep thought as he stares at the newspaper. When he sees me, he announces abruptly, "Doris, there is something you need to know. Your mother left this morning and was too upset to wake you to say goodbye."

"Thanks for the bulletin, Papi."

I stare at him while trying to swallow the large lump in my throat. He could have let me sit down first. He's wearing his pajama bottoms and a T-shirt with his band's name—¡Caliente! ¡Caliente!—that prominently features their motto, "It doesn't get hotter than this," and a silly drawing of a guitar on fire. After what feels like a century of ignoring my eyes' daggers, and my silence, he finally looks up from his paper, but doesn't even seem to notice my crumbling face.

"Where is she?"

"She has gone for a while." The way he says the words, like

someone trying not to say too much, makes me feel cold all over. He folds and refolds the newspaper.

"Where is she?" I hear the whine in my own voice and feel the baseball-size lump in my throat throbbing—this means I'm going to start bawling like a baby any minute.

"*Hija*, your mother doesn't want me to say any more right now, just that she's okay. She called me when I was in the city with the Merry Widows and told me that she needs to get away. She needs time to herself, Doris. Can you trust me on this?"

No, I can't trust him on this! They are both playing games with me. I hate the way they treat me like an adult when it suits them, but keep me out of all their plots and plans.

"By herself?" I ask him, sarcasm creeping into my voice.

"She said she needs time *to* herself. Doris, you are fifteen, almost a woman. You know how to take care of yourself, and I'll be around as much as I can. Please, *mi amor* . . ." But I don't let him finish the sentence. I run up to the roof to be by myself, church forgotten. The pigeons are gone for the day, but at least I can count on them coming home at night. I let myself cry as much as I want. I guess I knew Mami was going to leave, but having my father actually say it was like being punched in the stomach.

"Where are you?" I scream the question up at the sky and then down at the sidewalk, where an old woman stops and looks up. I didn't know my voice carried so far.

* * *

4

After I scream and cry, I feel a bit saner, and I start thinking: Is it my fault that my parents' marriage has exploded—just like the junky band speakers that they blew up one night?

Although Mami has always played the quirky artist and diva, I don't think my parents are unhappy. My father seems content to be doing what he does most days. He makes plans for his bands. He writes songs about an island that is real only in his dreams, about women who are much more beautiful than the ones he knows. He talks to me about the future. His idea is that I will get an education and make a life away from the barrio. He wants *me* to be the one to fly the furthest because I am smart and practical. He thinks I should switch to a Catholic high school, and maybe go to college. He thinks that I will be *saved* from the bad influences of the barrio through an education, become a good, successful Latina— whatever that means.

¡Caliente! ¡Caliente! (most people forget the second *caliente*, which upsets my father, who gave it two names for a reason—he wants it said like you just got burned: hot! hot!) is one of two bands my father co-manages. He is also the drummer. The other one is an all-woman polka group called the Merry Widows. But he only travels with ¡Caliente! I know he prefers to stay near home. He has his fan base here. Or maybe he wanted to stay home for my mother, who, on bad days, acted like our apartment was a cage. She talked about time running out. At one point, she wanted me to take voice lessons and to sing some duets with her. She kept talking about the School of Performing Arts. She thought we could be famous as a mother/daughter singing team. But the more she tried to persuade me, the less I liked the idea.

I finally lost it, and informed them that I was not their property, that I sing only when I want to. I particularly didn't want to sing in a salsa band to a bunch of loud people drinking rum all night long and then go home to sleep the day away and dream of fame and fortune.

To clear my head of all my parents' mumbo jumbo, I began going to the roof, where I've taken up the care and feeding of Doña Iris's pigeons. Their lives make sense to me. Birds know the time by instinct: when it's time for their coops to be opened, when to fly, and when to come home and eat the food I set out for them. The couples go to their own little apartments after a day of flying. They have a purpose for each hour.

Now, up on the roof, the sky seems close enough to touch. I imagine that just beyond the blue is the place where dreams are stored, and the closer you get to them, the easier it is to call them into your head. If I could get away with it, I'd make myself a place to live up here. It would be so sweet to fall asleep listening to the soft cooing of the pigeons, then to wake to a new day, free of walls.

I am the not-beautiful, not-really-ugly only child of *salseros*. But, unlike my parents, I am not musically *obsessed*, although I can sing almost as well as my mother.

And I am a medium. This is not my size in T-shirts. It means that I have dreams that show me things no one else knows. And I can tell a lot about a person just by being in the same room. None of my friends know this about me. I only found out myself when our neighbor, Doña Iris, the local oracle and, when I was little, my sometime babysitter, told me I had *facultades*. Having *facultades* means that a person has the potential to receive the gift of clairvoyance. You have to train yourself to accept it; if you don't, then your talent will disappear. Doña Iris said my mother did just that, wasted her own spiritual talent by focusing on singing trivial songs about people falling in and out of love. "God is generous, Doris, but he's not going to give someone two gifts at once," Doña Iris said when I asked whether my mother had *facultades*, too: "Your mother chose singing instead of dreaming, and He said, Okay, girl, if that's what you want, but you can't have both. Not in equal measure, you can't."

Doña Iris went on speaking. "Want to know all there is to know about *El Amor*?" I thought she was asking me a question, but she was only making a point. "You won't learn it from listening to silly songs, or even from reading psychology books. *Love* with a capital L happens to be a different thing for every single human being. So if you want to know what *El Amor* is, wait your turn. If you are lucky, you won't have to ask."

So Doña Iris talked me into it. I gave up practicing my singing and started concentrating on my other gift, the one my mother had rejected. What's singing compared to conference calls with the dead?

My mother does not like Doña Iris much, but my father

does. Mami calls her La Bruja, the witch, and says that the only reason that she can see into the future is because she snoops around our building all day long and knows everybody's personal business. Still, she had no choice when it came to a babysitter for me; there was no one else to stay with me the nights my parents were away.

These days, I don't spend much time with Doña Iris. She has started to go senile, especially since her buddy, Don Pichón, died. But lately I've been thinking about the things she said about my "gift."

I hear my mother's voice when I look through my boxes of what she called "souvenirs": calendars, posters, wedding and baptism favors, napkins with pictures of old couples celebrating their fiftieth anniversaries—all kinds of stuff she brought home to me as a sort of show-and-tell, to illustrate her stories of where she'd been performing and the people she had met. These were my good-night stories when I was little. In my mind, I'd fly to those parties as she spoke, and she'd make me laugh with her imitations of the drunk father of the bride, or the birthday girl at a fancy *quinceañera* spilling punch on her thousand-dollar gown.

The day my mother left, I started to have strange dreams at night, dreams where I *feel* my mother's presence in the room, smell her perfume, and hear her voice. It takes me a while to convince myself that it's all in my head.

I also start dreaming about flying, but these are daydreams. While I scrub the roof of bird poop and human trash—beer bottles, candy wrappers, a roach here and there—I imagine what it'd be like to fly over the city toward the ocean. While I wait for my mother to come home, and for my father to stay around long enough to make a plan for the future, I try to make my own flight plan.

In the meantime, I take care of the birds. It's the deal I make with myself this crazy spring when both my parents have gone nuts: I'll stay cool for a while, at least until school ends. I'll keep the apartment from turning into a dump and take care of the birds. After that, I don't know. Maybe I'll fly away, too.

2

I tell myself that my mother will come back to us. And I halfway believe it, too.

When I tell Papi I think she is just playing a game with us, he looks at me with faraway eyes that are already beginning to erase her image and says: "Don't talk about things you don't know anything about."

What didn't I know about in our apartment? Our rooms, theirs and mine, share a very thin wall. And there isn't anything wrong with my ears—just with my head maybe for trying to live with a couple of wacko musicians. I always know when they've had a fight and when they make up. They're noisy people.

This year started out really well for them. They had played gigs all over town. ¡Caliente! was still a favorite band for Latino parties of all kinds. And the Merry Widows were also beginning to show a profit. Then my mother found out about the diminishing savings account. This was not the first time my father's loose grip on *el dinero* had disrupted our family life. But this time my mother refused to forgive him. It had something to do with my future and her career, though it wasn't clear what the real problem was. I kept hearing her say my name through the wall.

"Not a baby anymore. She is a mature young woman. Soon she'll spread her wings," I heard her say one night. Her words apparently reminded Papi of the pigeons, and the next thing I heard was the door slamming and him running up the stairs to the roof. She screamed after him: "*¡Si yo tuviera alas!*" "If I had wings" became her theme song. But even normal things also seemed to get to Mami in a big way. She was always complaining that she was tired, that her head hurt. I thought that she was finding new ways to tell Papi and me that she was sick of us.

Now that I think of it, my mother has always been a loaded gun waiting to go off, or maybe a firecracker announcing the start of a fiesta, I still haven't decided which. My grandmother once told me that ever since her pretty Claribel (a name my mother hates) was a little girl, she knew two things about herself: that she was good-looking and that she could sing. Mami had been born in a barrio in the Bronx, but when her father died unexpectedly of a heart attack, she had gone back to Puerto Rico so her mother could be near her extended family. That's when my father had come into the picture. He had discovered Mami singing at a tourist hotel in San Juan while he was on vacation there. My parents' meeting had been a business deal at first sight. He had changed professions that same week, reinventing himself from wandering musician and ladies' man to Claribel's manager. The young singer was ready to conquer Nueva York. In my father she saw her ticket to the big time. Papi had been impressed by the lovely and talented Claribel Martínez López Colón and convinced her to marry him, even though his territory was not the Nueva York of her dreams, but a city across the Hudson River—Paterson, New Jersey. He had convinced her that New Jersey was the New World for Latinos, who were overflowing from the Bronx and creating new barrios (and new business opportunities) in the Garden State. Abuela was not happy about giving her daughter up to the fast-talking young entrepreneur, but being wise, she finally understood that her daughter's dreams had now relocated back to the mainland. So she helped to arrange a hasty but proper wedding for her Claribel. In time, Papi had become a successful manager of two bands, a semidevoted husband and father, and a very ambitious businessman, always looking for the big break.

I had come along uninvited during the second year they were married. They carried me in a basket to their gigs and put me on tables while they did their shows. There was always someone to watch me. I was the centerpiece nobody noticed unless I screamed louder than the band played. So when I got old enough to stay home, I did. Doña Iris was nutty, but she was always sweet and loving to me. And at least she kept it quiet around her place. I never did like parties much—I guess it has to do with a fiesta being a way of life for my family. Everything gets old, even partying, when you do it all the time.

* * *

Fifteen years later—and it's time for my own *quinceañera* party. Can it be that it was only a month ago they were talking me up, telling me over and over, *Doris, you are almost a woman. Congratulations.*

Papi is in his gray business suit, badly matched with a tie-dyed Jerry Garcia tie. (He's not into the retro look. He really thinks he's dressed in up-to-the-minute fashion in gold and royal blue.) He is tapping his fingers on his worn-out missal. Mami is in her most "conservative" suit, the one that converts into a strapless evening dress when she removes the jacket. She is adjusting the red shawl over my shoulders. I am a little irritated by her attentions, wishing I had dressed like a good Catholic girl, maybe in a brown, knee-length skirt, long-sleeved white button-down blouse, and loafers with socks, instead of making a fashion statement—that would have been more of a surprise to her. Too late—I'm stuck in my own game when I really just wanted to show her how silly her diva act is.

"You're not going to let her wear that ridiculous getup to church, are you?" Papi's tone is really a plea. Please, he is saying with his big brown eyes, please, *mi amor*, do something about this.

But Mami doesn't answer. She just smiles big, her *ojos negros*, eyes as black as onyx, showing white all around in mock surprise at his objections—what he calls her wicked witch look. But it's not always amusing when she's in a trickster mood; he and I both know this. When the wicked witch takes over, Mami is likely to do anything. Once she threw a costume party at the Caribbean Moon, where everyone had to dress up and act like their husband, wife, or significant other. Did that cause an uproar! She told me that no one really knows how another person sees them until you show them. It had been quite a revelation to watch people "seeing" themselves through their loved one's eyes. Let's just say it was not a party people talked about afterward, at least not in front of us.

Another time, on the spur of the moment, she just took off to see her mother on the island without telling us. After Papi and I had practically gone mad with worry, Abuela finally called to say that Claribel was with her, "taking a break." We were supposed to understand that Mami had an "artistic temperament." My mother is not a bad person, and I believe she loves us, but she thinks everyone should accept that as an artist she has special needs. But I think artists should have some common sense, too. Doesn't she realize I need her at home?

I remember that on the day of my *quinceañera* she just seemed to want to indulge herself and infuriate me.

"We're ready," she says, as she drapes a long black lace mantilla over her head and shoulders. This is strictly for its dramatic effect, since the Catholic church no longer requires that women cover their heads at Mass. She looks like she's walking down the red carpet, posing for the paparazzi, as she whirls by me out the door. She's short, only five feet tall, but in heels and wearing tight clothes she is as glamorous as a

14

movie star, and she knows it. Papi looks me over once more, sighs, and follows me outside.

A couple of our stuffier neighbors are out on the stoop waiting to check us out. They even brought their snacks, tasty plantain chips and Cokes—apparently it takes a lot of carbohydrates and sugar to snoop and gossip. We are the only people in show business they know and they are trying to decide whether we're respectable. Frankly, given my childhood, I have a hard time telling normal from strange myself. For example, my parents go to church, but they don't let religion interfere with their lives. It's just part of what they learned they were supposed to do on Sundays. By Monday they have forgotten what the old padre said about "doing unto others" and all the Golden Rule stuff about love and peace, and they go back to arguing and doing unto each other what they wouldn't want done unto them.

Papi and I step into the sunlight, and I catch him shaking his head in despair as he checks out my costume in full daylight.

I decide I must look like a birthday cake in my scarlet Mexican skirt and puff-sleeved embroidered poet's shirt; I'm all white frosting and red candy flowers. I like settling into my crinolines, spreading them out over the entire seat of the car. They smell a little musty—I picked them up at the thrift store last week and forgot to wash them. I sit in the front passenger seat just to make Mami mad.

"Dorita, *por favor*." She imperiously orders me out of her seat. She also pinches her nose as I slide past her. As soon as she's in the car, she begins to put on lipstick. She twists the rearview mirror all the way to her side of the car. Papi takes his time adjusting his seat belt. He is really just waiting for her to give him control of the vehicle. She will not put on her seat belt until she has finished "touching up" her makeup, and he will not start the car until we are both buckled up. I wait until he barks at me: "Seat belt, seat belt!" He is hoping Mami will respond to his command, too. She doesn't. Her hair has to be fluffed up first, and the mantilla arranged just right over her head and shoulders.

It takes Papi several long minutes and a lot of twisting and turning to readjust the mirror for driving again. Mami watches him with the devil in her eyes. I see her squeezing his plump thigh when he finally succeeds in making all the necessary preparations for the five-minute drive to Queen of Heaven. We could walk, but I think he's afraid Mami and I will cause a traffic accident. Besides, he likes making a big entrance in the same church where he made his communion decades ago, when it was mostly an Irish, Italian, and Polish neighborhood and he was one of the few Latinos.

"Seat belts?" Papi calls out again.

"Yes!" both of us yell out at the top of our lungs.

And we're off to pay for our sins of the week by sitting through a Mass said bilingually in Spanish and English, so that the old neighborhood residents who are still hanging on to their roots here, and the new Puerto Rican, Dominican, Salvadoran, Ecuadorian, Colombian, and who knows what other Spanish-speaking people, will all hear the words of our multicultural God. Now, after the wave of new immigrants, their church sits in the middle of a Latino parish. Mami says even the saints have gotten darker since the browning of the city that began when she returned to the States. That means the service lasts twice as long, and it drives me crazy to hear things repeated, since I understand both languages. It's like going to an American movie dubbed in Spanish: I keep reading the actors' lips and hearing them talk out of sync in another language. Crazy.

The part I love about the Mass is Mami's voice rising like an angel's over the whole congregation when we sing the hymns. She becomes a divine creature when she sings a song she loves, closing her eyes tight and forgetting that her mascara will run with the tears that will come when she really gets into the words. She scrunches her face in an effort to make the Ave Maria rise all the way to the baby in Mary's lap on the ceiling fresco.

"God be with you," Father Connolly intones after the echoes of Mami's high notes have subsided and the congregation is again his.

"*Y con tu espíritu,*" "And with you," everyone says at once after answering both him and his interpreter, Mrs. Dorset, a retired Spanish teacher who now relies on a dictionary for translations and sometimes says very bizarre things. That Sunday she tells us in Spanish that we must not forget to wear better-fitting undergarments to church, when Father Connolly's message is really to remind the women (particularly Mami and me) to dress more modestly for Mass. Mami nearly passes out from holding back a fit of laughter. Papi escorts her outside, pretending that she is choking on something, but her voice carries, and to cover up the hysterical laughter, Father Connolly skips a few pages of the missal and hurries into an unscheduled bilingual chorus of the Alleluia. It's my mother's kind of day.

But this is supposed to be *my* special day, my *quinceañera*. It turns out to be special all right—but not the way I expected. I can see it in vivid detail—like a movie in my mind.

On the wall of El Lechón y el Gallo restaurant there is a giant mural of a fat pink pig facing off with a cocky rooster while a man with a knife and fork looks them over with a malicious grin on his face. This is "early Latino immigrant" decor done by the owner himself, Don Gaspar. He and his plump wife are hanging streamers and balloons when we arrive, all-purpose decorations that go up for all celebrations.

"*Feliz cumpleaños* and happy birthday, too!" Don Gaspar yells at me across the room. There is clapping and more yelling from two waitresses stuffed into starched black-and-white maid's uniforms. The restaurant is closed today for a wedding. Don Gaspar and Doña Celia are serving us a birthday lunch as a special favor to my parents, who, in return, will play an extra hour at the wedding reception immediately following my so-called *quinceañera* party.

We are just sitting down to our *sopa de pollo* and pork fritters when we hear Geraldo, ¡Caliente! ¡Caliente!'s co-manager, scream in an angry tone, "Who the hell asked *you* here?"

"I'm here to talk to the boss, you moron. And I would be working this gig, if you weren't such a hog." It's Greta Lipsky, the accordion player for the Merry Widows, who is batting down the many layers of her polka-dotted dress that seem to have flared up around her tail like an angry chicken's feathers. She's glaring at Geraldo, who is straightening his pencil-thin tie and acting like a Mafia boss whose territory has been invaded by a rival gang. She starts toward him, and as he scurries to the kitchen she follows, her tail feathers shaking in anger.

There are the sounds of a scuffle, and both my parents take off toward the kitchen. The four of them emerge moments later into the dining room wearing transformed faces. Papi is flushed, wiping his sweaty face with his hanky. Mami is smiling calmly. It is her stage personality. *Stay calm even if they throw tomatoes at you.* Geraldo struts in behind her. In his streamlined black suit and shiny black Italian slip-ons, he looks like a bad imitation of a gangster. *El Gallito*, the little rooster, is what my father calls him.

"Can we just sit down and talk business here?" Papi pulls out two chairs for the ladies simultaneously. He points to a chair for Geraldo across the table from Greta's. He is being the smooth diplomat now. My birthday forgotten, Greta explains that she's found out that Geraldo has been stealing potential business from the Widows by going behind Papi's back and "seducing" certain women "who shall remain nameless" to hire ¡Caliente! She tosses a meaningful look in the direction of Doña Celia, who at that moment is poised on a short ladder hanging strips of white crepe paper from one end of the room, still decorating for the wedding while we "celebrate" my birthday. Don Gaspar is holding the ladder steady for her. She must be at least forty, with a butt big enough to serve a full-course meal on. But I notice that Geraldo is staring at her, or at least at part of her, and that Papi is also, but only when he is forced by Greta to take note of the woman. I gag on a stringy piece of chicken in my soup.

"Spit it out, Doris!" My mother is pounding my back. "Doris, are you okay?"

Through watery eyes I nod at Mami. She stares at me, and I know she is trying to read my mind. Although she makes fun of Doña Iris's fortune-telling, she claims that she can tell what's on people's minds as well as La Bruja, without all the hocus-pocus. It's called face-reading, she has told me. Eyes, mouth, and even eyebrows reveal a person's thoughts.

Now, chin cupped in her hand, Mami is intently studying Geraldo and Greta. Later, she will tell Papi which one of them is lying. It will be the woman. It always is. My mother hates female competition.

"*Está mintiendo*. She is a liar," Geraldo says in a calm voice. But I notice that his bottom lip is trembling and he seems to have developed a slight tic in his right eye.

"Let's speak in English, please, out of respect for the company." My father insists that business be conducted out loud in English, since he knows how tricky nonverbal signals can get among his musicians. A sly look can make or ruin a deal. Mami will switch back and forth from English to Spanish with us. But she says she dreams only in Spanish.

"Or Polish—how about if we talk in Polish?" Geraldo smiles his big-tooth wolf smile.

"You idiot!" Greta is up, a red-faced volcano rising from her layers of polka-dotted cotton and lace. She tosses a pork fritter at Geraldo, who catches it and lasciviously licks it before wolfing it down. Greta complains that ¡Caliente! ¡Caliente! is asked to play at Polish weddings more often than the Polish Merry Widows. This just doesn't make sense to Greta.

"Greta, Greta, Greta." Papi is trying to coax the furious woman back down to her chair by taking her elbow and pulling. Instead, she falls on his lap, the chair breaks under their considerable combined weight, and Mami, unable to restrain herself, begins laughing and clapping. Doña Celia cries, "*¡Ay Bendito!* Heaven help us!" when she sees what is happening to her property. A crowd gathers around the spectacle of Greta attempting to lift her bulk off Papi, while he is trying, without success, to push her off his chest.

Geraldo winks at Mami, pinches my cheek, and has disappeared into the background by the time we disentangle my poor gasping father from Greta. I try to regain my self-respect by sitting at the table and eating my slice of ultra-sweet chocolate cake as if all this were just part of the family show. It's time for Mami to get ready for her performance. She gives me an absent-minded kiss. *Feliz cumpleaños*, I say to myself. Happy birthday to me. And many more. My party is over.

Guests start to arrive and then when the newlyweds

appear at the reception, I can see why Greta thought the Merry Widows had a chance at this gig. The groom is Terrence "the Terror" Sandinsky, a reformed Romeo and the ex-boyfriend of several of the Widows, including Greta. His bride is my former backup babysitter, the new Teresa Rosario Gonzalez-Sandinsky. On the rare occasions when Doña Iris was sick, Teresa took over my care and feeding. She and Greta glare at each other across the room. If looks could kill, the body count in that room would be at least two. It's my guess that Greta wants to strut her stuff one last time in front of her former lover. That's why she wanted the gig so bad.

The first set begins. There is no other way to say it: when she is onstage, Mami is *possessed* by the music. Different parts of her body come alive to the salsa rhythms until she is what Papi calls a Puerto Rican tornado.

Mami puts on the face of romantic ecstasy as she sings the old Puerto Rican standards with the saucy lyrics. Soon her hips take on a life of their own and she's all over the place. Papi claims that if she could cook as well as she dances salsa and mambos, she'd be the ideal Latina wife.

"Their kids will probably come out spotted like Dalmatians. He is *so* white." Mami laughs as she sits down for a break while the band plays a waltz for the Gonzalez-Sandinskys.

When the time for her next set begins, my mother walks onto the stage and opens her mouth to sing, but instead she cries out and clutches her chest, an agonized expression on her face as she falls to her knees. The musicians stop playing; it sounds like someone has unplugged a jukebox and the record has come to a slow halt. My father and I run toward her, but Geraldo has already picked Mami up in his arms and we have to run after him to the kitchen.

"I'm okay," she keeps saying. She stands up, looking pale and shaky. "I am fine. Just got a cramp."

"You shouldn't eat and then dance like that, it's just like swimming," says Mrs. Sandinsky, the groom's mother, a woman with yellow hair and a pear-shaped body smothered in layers of blue satin.

The kitchen is now packed with a dozen overdressed, sweaty people.

"Please, please, let's give her a little room." Papi is trying to get people to go back to their tables. I am trying to get past Geraldo to my mother. I push him away and put my arms around my mother's trembling shoulders. I am really scared.

"Doris, listen. I'm fine, okay? Just get your father to say the band will be back in fifteen."

"Mami, are you sure? We could just have Geraldo sing today." He has an okay voice, although it's nothing to brag about.

Both Mami and Geraldo laugh at my suggestion. I don't like the sound of their laughter together. There is something intimate about it, like when two people share a secret joke.

"*Niña*, nobody who has heard your mama sing will settle for me."

"You could just shake your booty for the ladies." I can't help myself. I know it's the wrong time to snap at Geraldo, with my sick mother holding on to his skinny arm.

"*Niña*, please. I just need to rest a few minutes. Go back to the table and act normal, *por favor*. We don't want to ruin the party. Go on, I'll be in soon."

"That may be too much to ask of me, but I'll try." Although I'm worried about her, I'm angry, too. I've been dismissed like a child. It's my fifteenth birthday! Doesn't anyone remember this little fact?

For a moment I watch Geraldo putting his tacky suit jacket over my mother's shoulders and leading her outside for some fresh air. Then, wiping my tears and putting on a fake smile, I head out of the overheated kitchen back to the table. People are eating cake and drinking rum-spiked punch. I notice that the Sandinskys and the Gonzalezes are grouped by family allegiance, or is it by color? Anyway, only the head table is integrated and that's because each seat has a name tag. Gonzalez. Sandinsky. Gonzalez. Gonzalez. Sandinsky and Gonzalez-Sandinsky. Just like at Mass, it helps to know both languages. I keep looking back at the kitchen door. The crowd is making restless noises.

"Where's the band?" the groom's father, a red-faced man who is wider than he is tall, yells out. He is obviously drunk, and his wife, who is Mrs. Lean to his Mr. Fat, pulls the tails of his tux, trying to make him shut up. "I just wanna know where the hot saucy singer is!" He means to say the *salsa singer*. He is turning red in the face.

I watch my father pat Greta on her plump shoulder and make his way toward the new disturbance. He has his smile of peace-making set firmly on his face. Mami likes to make fun of what Papi calls his diplomatic skills. "Without which," he reminds her, "I could not survive the minority wars." The constant bickering between his bands is what he is talking about. They both want to work, and it's no use explaining to the Merry Widows that he just can't get them as many gigs as he can ¡Caliente! ¡Caliente! Even Latinos who cannot afford to pay the rent will still dish out money for live music at one of their many celebrations.

Grand finale: Mami sashays into the reception, still pale, but glamorous in fresh makeup. She is wearing a new outfit, what she has christened her salsa dress, the gold, skin-tight strapless number with the dancing glass beads hanging from it in strategic places, so that when she moves, she is shooting sparks of light in every direction.

She sends me a kiss through the air—must watch that lipstick. It's showtime again.

After her collapse at the wedding party, the changes in my mother became very noticeable, at least to me; I never heard Papi say a word about it, not even *¿Qué pasa?* She moped around the apartment, like what Doña Iris calls a lost soul, *una alma perdida.* She got a lot of calls from Geraldo, too. When I answered the phone, I would always tell him she was asleep, but most times she picked up the extension in her room. She and Papi started doing a lot of closed-door arguing. I could always tell they were arguing by the tone that rose and fell like thunder before a storm.

I used all my mind-reading tricks to figure out what was going on. Mami knew it, too, that I was trying to get into her head, and she tried to block me. She also spent a lot of time in her room, claiming she was always tired. But I knew that she was hiding from me. To look into people's minds, you really have to watch them and look into their eyes. Eyes don't lie. That's what both Doña Iris and Mami herself have told me.

And so, even before she actually left, she was not really here. And I am getting ready for the day when I will remember her like a dream.

3

D oris! Hey, you coming out to say goodbye, or what?"
It's my father. I knew he was going to call me out of
my room by six a.m., so I woke up like clockwork at a quarter
till. My father and the salsa band are off for a weekend gig in
the Poconos, minus Mami. She has been gone for three weeks
now. "Coming!" I yell.

Papi is laying the emergency kit out for me on our kitchen
table. Phone numbers, cash for food, a credit card "for emergency use only," a sealed envelope with "Doris" written on
it—instructions for me should he die in a fiery crash caused
by the hard-drinking bus driver whom Papi cannot fire
because he is the best trumpet player in the business.

"*Mi amor*, are you sure you gonna be okay?"

He always asks me that. I've been taking care of myself
for years, even when Mami was around. After I became convinced that the whole world smelled like the stale beer and
cigarette butts in the clubs they played, I asked, no, begged, to
be allowed to stay alone in our apartment while they were out

playing gigs. I'd have the TV to myself and uncensored reading time. The price I paid for the privilege was doing all the housework.

My father is nodding at everything I say, but I can see that he's deep into himself. Is he missing Mami, or is there already somebody new? Though he fools around some, I think he still loves her. I just don't think he'll wait forever. I stay quiet and let him think. The smell of her White Diamonds perfume is still on everything. I've made sure of that. I watch him take out what he thinks is his handkerchief to wipe his always-sweaty forehead, but it's one of her red gloves (I sprayed it with White Diamonds, too). Mami has this bad habit of stashing her things anywhere that's convenient to her; any pocket she finds in a closet will do. I have gone to school carrying her keys more than once, only to be called down to the office where my mother, still wearing the sequined dress from last night's show, is waiting for me to give her the key to our apartment.

"I'm late," Papi says, gulping down the last of his coffee. He seems so nervous that I go over and hug his neck. He smells like coffee and cigarettes and Mami's perfume.

"I'll be fine, Papi. You better get going or Sánchez will have to drive at more than the speed of light to get the band there on time." He looks at me with those tragically sad brown eyes that women seem to find so attractive. He wants to hear an "I'll take care of everything." He wants me to do something about the situation with Mami. He wants her home to worry about me so that he can concentrate on business.

"Doris?" He turns back at the door and gives me a pleading look. "Do you mind not wearing your mother's stage costumes around the house?"

I nod. But I like putting on her dresses, although I try to avoid the ones with beads, feathers, and sequins. One night I slept in one of them and woke up looking like I had chicken pox, I had scratched myself so much. But today I'm wearing an emerald-green velvet strapless gown that makes me feel like I am in a permanent bear hug.

When I wore it to school last week, I had put a denim jacket over it so that my naked shoulders wouldn't give any of my teachers a brain hemorrhage, but I was sent home to change anyway.

"Trashy appearance. Unsuitable attire. Dress-code violation." These were a few of the choice phrases I recall from my afternoon of solitary confinement in the assistant principal's office. Only my friend Arturo appreciates my new fashion statements. He says I look spectacular.

"Dream Girl. Hot Latina Babe. Salsa Queen on Wheels."

I love Arturo.

Later that afternoon, desperate to understand why my mother had to leave us to be happy, I decide I can use a little supernatural help. So I go up to the roof to tell Doña Iris about my dreams. Her specialties are palm reading, telling fortunes with cards, and performing an occasional séance. She says that these days, reading minds and interpreting dreams is hard on her poor tired brain.

But she listens very carefully to what I say while she stares over the buildings at the horizon in a sort of trance. Then she begins to talk as if I weren't there.

"To dream of a caged bird means that your soul is trapped. To dream of a free bird that circles and doesn't alight means that you are lost and confused. You must pay attention to the direction in which the bird in your dream flies. If he is plunging, you must beware of danger closing in on you; if he is ascending, it may mean that you wish to see or to know everything at once, like a bird sees the world. It is good to dream of a pleasant flight that comes to an end." I look up to see Martha, the leader of the pigeons, flying in, focusing on her home. As she circles closer, we see that she is bringing us something in her beak.

Martha alights a bit unsteadily on the cage roof. We approach her slowly so as not to frighten her away. I take Martha in my open hands, folding her wings under, the way the bird book said it should be done. Her whole little body beats like a heart in my hands. I take the strip of paper from her beak as I place her inside the coop. It's some sort of Chinese fortune cookie message decorated with a gold dragon. The gold is probably what had attracted Martha's eye. I hand Doña Iris the slip of paper.

"In dreams, the dragon is a symbol for the urge to fly, and to find a safe nest. It is both a bird of the sky and a snake of the earth. The warrior is always pursuing it, but the beast almost always escapes and goes to hide in the most secret place," says Doña Iris, still in her staring trance.

So the dragon is half bird and half snake. This makes a weird kind of sense to me. To have dragon powers, you have to be like both creatures, at least in your thinking; you have to be able to crawl *and* fly.

Although by now I am a little tired of Doña Iris's prophetic proclamations, I have to ask her what she means by "the most secret place."

"Both dragon and bird always return to their nest," she says in a stern tone that means she has nothing more to say on the subject. She asks me to help her go down the stairs to her apartment. "I am tired, *hija*. My legs are hurting. And I miss my dear friend Juan Pablo today." The old woman's mind starts to really wander then. All the way to her apartment, she keeps talking as if I were her boyfriend, the one we had all called Don Pichón, the late bird man of our building.

I remember a day, a few years ago, when I had snuck up behind her and Don Juan Pablo, alias Don Pichón, to watch the pigeons come back at sundown. Don Pichón and Doña Iris had been inseparable, two crazy old people living next door to each other for almost fifty years. After World War II, Don Pichón had come back obsessed with homing pigeons. He claimed that he had personally seen G.I. Joe—the most famous messenger pigeon of them all. He told the story about a thousand times a year. The bird supposedly flew under heavy fire for twenty miles to deliver a message for air support to Allied troops. Don Pichón had a newspaper clipping, which I always thought had been faked, that shows this big-chested pigeon with a bullet-shaped capsule strapped to his back. Under it a headline: G.I. JOE GETS MEDAL FOR GALLANTRY FROM BRITS. The year scribbled on the yellow paper was 1946.

The rumor in our barrio was that Don Pichón had lost something in the war, and I suspected it had been a few thousand brain cells. He lived on his disability pension all his life. The only thing he spent money on was his birds. No one I knew in our building remembered a time when Don Pichón and his birds had not occupied one fourth of our roof. Once in a while someone's mother tried to get the "filthy rats with wings" removed, but all the other tenants always rallied around the old guy and bought him a little more time. My father even gave him cash every month for pigeon supplies. Not that he cared about the birds that much; it's just that Papi has a soft heart. His wallet is always open. He knew that I knew about the money, and that I knew that Mami wasn't supposed to know. He reminded me that Don Pichón was a war hero, one of the last ones still around. It was because of Papi that I got involved in taking care of the birds with Doña Iris.

Needless to say, Don Pichón had been the butt of a lot of jokes by my friends. And the jokes began to rub off on me, sticking to me like feathers. Some little kids in our building started calling me the "bird girl." I didn't care. I liked to watch the pigeons take off and land. I would never admit it to anyone, because they would think it's too cheesy, but it's a weird and wonderful sight to see those birds at sunset making their long flight over the city toward home. Then they'd circle slowly over the roof where Don Pichón, usually accompanied by the ever-yakking Doña Iris, would be standing, looking up at the sky as if for a vision of Mary and a host of angels. Don Pichón's wrinkled old face would always break into an ecstatic grin at the sight of his birds flying toward him. I mean he almost danced, it made him so happy to see his birds returning. They seemed to use his snow-white head as a marker for home: they alighted like little winged soldiers all around and on him. And Martha, his precious champion, almost always brought back something she'd drop in front of him before entering the cage. These bits and pieces of string, foil, paper, tinsel, or anything she could carry in her beak, preferably yellow or gold, were not material for nesting. Don Pichón had told me that females rarely contribute to nest-building.

"Iris, what do you think this is? Looks like Christmas tree stuff." Don Pichón would turn the tinsel over and over in his tobacco-stained fingers.

Like a teacher about to lecture to a class, Doña Iris would take the bit of gold foil in her hands, examine it through squinting eyes, and begin making up some outrageous story about a poor child who had not had a Christmas tree that year but who had found one that had been tossed out in an alley or something, somehow missed by the garbage collectors— and this kid would take the tinsel off the tree so that next year she could decorate her own tree.

"And how did Martha get it?" Don Pichón's eyes would

be wide by then. He was awed by the fantasy, caught in the web of tales the old woman was spinning.

"Well, my dear, the girl obviously dropped some on her way home."

"Where do you suppose she lives?"

"Could be anywhere. But I'd say not far. I would guess this kid lives somewhere in this neighborhood."

"I'm going to watch Martha real close from now on and see if she lands anywhere around here before she comes home."

"You do that, Juan Pablo. Martha will tell us where the child lives."

"Poor kid." Don Pichón would now be inside the loft, where no one else was allowed, making sure all the bowls were filled with seed and that none of the excitable birds had overturned their water. Then he and Doña Iris would climb down the steps of the roof holding hands, and go to their separate apartments.

I'd be on the other side of the roof, under an overhang. It was my secret place where I came to watch the birds early, before school, and at sunset, after my parents had left for their gigs. I didn't have to explain my whereabouts to anyone. The pigeons and the stories made the roof a sort of magical place for me. Don Pichón and Doña Iris were my mentors and guides, a good witch and a sorcerer, who were teaching me magic through their stories; and, in my mind, the birds were all princes and princesses under a spell. I had come to help decipher Martha's messages—those messages were the key to reversing the spell.

Now I try to understand what it's like to lose someone you love by watching Doña Iris. Before Mami left, I had lost only one person—my boyfriend Danny. We broke up because he wanted to play basketball more than he wanted to be with me. I thought of him for a while, but it's not the same as missing my mother, or like Doña Iris grieving for Don Pichón. Most days Doña Iris acts okay, but tonight she seems to miss his company in a very serious way. I know they were special friends—the last ones in our barrio from the first wave of Puerto Ricans to migrate from the island after World War II. All the others had either died, moved back to the island, or been put in nursing homes. But Don Pichón and Doña Iris had refused to budge. They thought of our building as their little *barrio* in the middle of the city. And now she is the only one left. I decide to walk her back to her place and leave.

She seems to wake up then. "*Dios te bendiga, hija,*" she says, giving me her blessing before going into her dark apartment. Then she turns around like she suddenly remembers something important and tells me in a deep, trembling, prophesying voice, the one she puts on when she's telling the believers what their future holds for them, "Doris, *hija*, when a bird fails to return home, you have two choices: you can go after her and lure her home with food, or you can let her go free. The only thing that takes away choice is death. You cannot bring the dead back home with promises or prayers. You can only keep them with you by remembering them at their best."

"Right, Doña Iris," I say. "*Gracias.* I'll keep this in mind. Get some rest now, okay?"

Then I guide her by her hand into the apartment, which smells of candles and rubbing alcohol. All her windows are wide open. Next to the roof, she has the best view of the city, all the chimneys she could ever want to see. I tell her to lock her door, and even kiss her cheek, which is lined with deep wrinkles, and feels papery, like an old treasure map.

Papi has been spending less and less time at home since he got back from his Poconos trip, so I am having breakfast alone and reading the bird manual I borrowed from Doña Iris when the phone rings. For a second I wonder if it is Mami, but when I pick it up, it's my guidance counselor, Mrs. Latham. She asks for my mother.

"She's not here right now." With a mouthful of Rice Krispies, it's easy to disguise my voice. "No, I am a neighbor here to check the place. No, I don't know when she'll be home. She's on a tour . . . Yes, I'll tell her to call you when she returns. Goodbye, Mrs. Latham."

Later, I go back into Mami's room and look through a pile of clothes on a chair. I choose a few items and lay them on the pink chenille bedspread. I slip into her skinny gold lamé pants. I dig through her T-shirt drawer for one with the map of the island of Puerto Rico on it and PUERTO RICO ME ENCANTA emblazoned over the chest in red, white, and blue.

"What shoes?" I ask myself, taking a look at the assortment lining her closet wall.

Black patent-leather sling-backs. The lamé pants are too tight for me to bend down, so I lie back on the bed with my feet up in the air to slip on the shoes. I am ready for another school day.

On the way out, I check our mailbox. In it is an envelope with my school address on it. I guess I have to open it, since neither of my caregivers is home. It is from Mrs. Latham and it says that Doris's "emotional withdrawal" concerns her. It also comments on my "increasingly unconventional taste in clothing." She wonders if there is someone at home to take care of things while they are out touring. Yes, there *is* a responsible person at home to take care of me.

I am here to do the job.

Our apartment is still empty when I come home after school, but the air is buzzing with troubles, just like the mosquitoes on the island. They can't be gotten rid of. You just have to wait until the hot, wet season ends.

I go into my parents' room and find Mami's bath and perfume collection. She is a bathtub junkie. She likes filling the big tub, which looks like a headless white whale, with steaming hot water, then pouring in her bath salts, beads, and oils. When somebody asks where she is, Papi will tell them, "She's cooking." It's her favorite way of coming back from the smoky, sweaty world of the Caribbean Moon. When she comes out, she smells like a tropical garden. In the winter, she'll sometimes share herself by rubbing our heads with her perfumed hands as she walks into the living room in her thick red-velour robe. It makes her look like a hibiscus flower in bloom. In summer, she is a daffodil, in her yellow Japanese kimono.

I take the jar labeled "Serenity" and head for the tub. On a hook, on the back of the bathroom door, the two robes hang limp and lifeless. I bring one of the kimono's sleeves to my nose and breathe deeply. Then *I* take a long bath. A few pigeon feathers that got caught in my hair fall into the water. Funny how beautiful white feathers turn an ugly gray so quickly, and how bad they smell when they're wet.

My mother always says that for her, being alive means that she has a song to sing every day. I am trying to remember the words to the songs she sang before our troubles began, but I can't call up a whole one, only bits and pieces. They all seem to be about love, tears, and broken hearts. Or flying away into a blue sky. *"Si yo tuviera alas"* was her favorite saying: if only I had wings. I remember some of the words to one, the one she sang to me when I was a child until I was sick of hearing it, "Cielito Lindo." It's a lullaby, but it doesn't make much sense except to a little kid being rocked to sleep by her *mamá.* It says something about that pretty birthmark you have next to your mouth, my pretty heavenly child, don't give it away to anyone else; it belongs to me. And then a chorus about how it's better to sing than to cry because singing makes your heart feel *alegre* again. Mami would get inspired by that lyric and sing so loud that we still get joking remarks from our neighbors about being *awakened* from a peaceful sleep by my mother's passionate rendition of the old island song that was supposed to be a lullaby.

Cielo also means sky, so maybe she was really singing about flying away. If only she had wings.

I find myself humming it under my breath while I try to relax in a tub full of Serenity. *Ay, ay, ay, ay, canta y no llores.*

4

This morning, again, I can't face school. Even though it's been almost two months since Mami left, I'm still going nuts. She has not written or called me once. I keep expecting her to walk in the door, hug me as if nothing had happened, take one of her hourlong baths, and start telling me about her "vacation." I've been home from school, sick for five days, and the school office keeps leaving messages about "Doris's continued absences." Fortunately Papi's never around, so I have been able to delete the messages before he hears them. Soon they'll send someone out to check up on me. I'm going back eventually, when I'm ready, though I'm so heavy with sadness that I can hardly drag myself around. I miss my mother. I am angry, too. I should be glad she's gone and done what she always wanted to do: get away from this old dreary barrio, follow her dream, blah, blah, blah. Or is she sick or in trouble, and doesn't want me to know?

I go up to the roof and throw the cage doors wide open. The birds fly off in a single wave of motion, as if they have a place to go, somewhere where they are expected. I drag my lounge chair behind a chimney stack and drift off to sleep in the morning sun.

In my dream, I look for my mother. I don't find her in the apartment, although I open each door and check every room. I don't find her in the little gravel plot we call a backyard where she sometimes sat with a glass of wine in her hand, laughing at the world with Papi. I don't find her in the old barrio where she sometimes liked to go visit people she met in church or on gigs. She isn't at Norma's House of Beauty getting her hair permed, or at Corazón's Café gossiping with the old lady; she isn't at Doña Blanquita's basement apartment getting her hand read, and, though I don't think she'd be there, I check the church, pew by pew, even the confessional boxes, which she isn't likely to hide in—she calls them coffins turned on their heads. But it is important that I look everywhere, so I climb to the bell tower of the church, knowing I will have to start off from a high place, and I fly over the dark Atlantic to my grandmother's house in Puerto Rico. I find all the doors locked and the houses empty, as if everyone in the world has suddenly disappeared.

I shoot out of the dark hole of this dream like a bullet and fall out of the folding chair where I had dozed off. Doña Iris says that letting the sun or moon shine on your face while you sleep will cause nightmares. And it has.

"*¿Qué pasa?*" I say aloud to no one. Sometimes my brain goes into Spanish during sleep, and it takes a strong cup of Bustelo coffee to tune back in to English.

¿Qué pasa? is the quintessential Puerto Rican question—
wassup?—and lately it has been popping into my mind, awake
or asleep. What is happening? That is the question. Also, why
is there a heavy weight like a rock on my chest all the time
now? Do I really miss her that much, or is it a *premonition*—a
new word I picked up in one of the books on mind-reading
I bought when I was interested in developing my skills as a
clairvoyant?

Papi spent the first few weeks after Mami left worrying
about—and trying to spend more "quality time" with—his
Dorita (this usually meant joining me for coffee in the morn-
ings, and making inane conversation while trying to keep
from falling asleep with a mouth full of Fruit Loops). Since
then, he is back to his old routine of sleeping until noon, and
staying at the Caribbean Moon all night when ¡Caliente! is
playing. He has found a *temporary* replacement singer, a
woman he met working in a hotel in the Poconos, half
Jewish, half Puerto Rican, named Margarita Goldblum. Papi
calls me from the club that afternoon to invite me to hear her
rehearse with the band. I agree only because he sounds a little
desperate. He even said, "*Por favor*, Doris. We will have a
little quality time together." Quality time, I think, at the
Caribbean Moon?

He and I sit in a back booth. The place smells like stale
everything, as usual. He stares at Ms. Goldblum the whole
time. In looks, she is the opposite of Mami. Goldblum is
stacked, muscular, built like a storm shelter, not small and

soft like Mami. She is taller than all the musicians in the group, and has a voice like a bullfrog on steroids. A deep one that carries. Papi says she doesn't need a microphone to blow away the audience.

"What about Mami?" I ask him after he finishes praising the new salsa singer.

"When she returns . . . she and Margarita can take turns singing. People like variety, you know? What do you think?" He is sounding a little like me when I want permission to do something. I hate it when parents do that to you—ask you to say it's okay for them to do things they feel guilty about.

I feel a little bit sorry for him. He does look like an abandoned puppy, but I don't want to hear about the woman replacing my mother in ¡Caliente!, so I decide to go home.

Our street is quiet. Everybody who has a normal life is at home with their families. I don't feel like being alone, so I go visit Arturo.

Arturo is usually alone in the apartment he shares with his mother. His stepfather went out one day for a six-pack of beer and never returned. Arturo likes it better now. He's a loner anyway. I'm practically his only close friend. But then the boy is an odd one. He hasn't decided what he is yet, so every so often, he tries on new identities. This week he refuses to talk. He is using sign language to communicate. It's okay with me. My brain has been so busy the last couple of months that a silent friend might be just what I need.

Arturo's apartment is in my building, but it might as well be in outer space. His mother lets him decorate it—I think she's just too tired to care what her place looks like. She has to work two jobs to make rent and bills, ten- or twelve-hour days. Arturo finds ways to help out. He is an assistant to the alterations woman at El Bazar, the clothing boutique in our barrio. He is mainly her "gofer." But she gives him all sorts of scraps of material that he uses in his art projects. He also gets to design the store window displays. It's his personal gallery. He escorts me to each of his openings: fall sale, winter sale, spring and summer sales. Best dressed mannequins in town. He "tans" the dummies with wood stain so they look more like El Bazar's Latina customers, although he can't do much about their anorexic plastic bodies. "Wonderbras help a little," he told me, "and a little foam padding in strategic places."

"That's good to know," I said, thinking that maybe he was giving me a hint.

I smell something unidentifiable cooking as I knock on his door (using the brass knocker he found in the trash, a lion's head with one glass eyeball missing, *el gato tuerto*, the one-eyed cat, my mother calls it every time we go by the apartment on our way to ours). Arturo opens the door wearing his coat of many colors, a sort of kimono he made from odd scraps of material.

"Thanks." I step inside into the latest decor. Silk scarves hang over the two lamps, casting a soft golden light on the futon he and his mother sit on during the day and where he sleeps at night. He's got a sort of tea party laid out on the coffee table. My eyes catch the setting—two cups, two plates, two of everything.

"I've come at a bad time." I start to turn around, but Arturo takes my elbow and shakes his head no.

He sits on the floor, on a pillow, and invites me to do the same. I know this is not just afternoon tea at Arturo's. He makes an unzipping motion across his lips.

"I'm glad you're here, Doris. I have a surprise planned for Mami. You can help me make it really special." I was going to ask him for more information, but he has zipped his lips again, and is pointing at the door. At that precise moment his mother walks in, looking more exhausted than I have ever seen anyone look.

She takes off her cashier's smock and hangs it on a hook, then kicks her shoes off. Besides working the register at the drugstore, she is also a cleaning woman in an office building uptown several nights a week. She looks at us like she's trying to figure out what's going on, then breathes deeply, and smiles.

"*Hola*, Doris."

"*Hola*, Doña Clara." I'm feeling like an intruder at this surprise party. I wonder whether I should leave. Again I start to go. "Stay, Doris. I just remembered. It's my birthday and Arturo—if my nose is right—has made a Japanese dinner for me. I followed my nose all the way upstairs. Let me take a shower and we can eat. Okay?"

She goes over and rubs Arturo's spiky hair and kisses him loudly on the cheek.

When she leaves the room, Arturo pulls a big yellow robe out of the coat closet and holds it open for me. We have to pretend that it is a kimono, but he wants me to dress for the party, too. It makes me think of my mother's real silk kimono. Then Arturo starts bringing out little dishes of noodles, rice, and pastry-type things that smell wonderful.

"Arturo, this is great. You made it all yourself?"

He nods.

"Can I look around until your mom comes out?" He makes a sweeping gesture with his arms that means *go ahead*. So I do.

I can tell he's glad that I'm interested in his weird creations. Most of the kids in the barrio laugh at his "art." But I am amazed by the papier-mâché masks that he makes. He brought one to school one day that looked so much like our bald principal, nerdish glasses and all, that our homeroom teacher threw a coat over it to keep kids from poking it with pencils or doing worse things to it.

I see that Arturo is back to his drawing, too. It's mostly sketches of the sky, with clouds, without clouds, at night. I recognize the views from the roof. His stepfather hated it when Arturo cooked, painted, or did anything the man considered feminine, and that was anything that did not involve power tools, heavy machinery, sweat, and cursing. Arturo often came to the roof just to get away from his stepfather's rampages against him and his mother.

"You need birds in your pictures, Arturo."

I look around. Everything has been freshly painted, and

even the old things look new. The walls of the living room are a deep green; the ceiling is blue, with foamy clouds sponged in. The floor is covered with a threadbare woven rug that someone probably threw out and Arturo salvaged. But it looks good here, makes an island in the middle of the room. I get close to it to see the design. I can almost make out the flowers and vines on it. My eyes are pulled from one color to another. It's amazing how it's all different, but it all goes together. Suddenly I feel almost happy in this room. It's a place where everything has been arranged with care. My parents are minimalists about our place. Neither one of them is much into decorating. It's like a hotel where they sleep and eat—their real home is the stage.

I go back and sit on the cushion. Arturo brings out a yellow teapot that smells as if roses were steaming in it. He knocks on his mother's bedroom door. She comes out in her flowered bathrobe, her hair still wet. Her face looks more relaxed, and she smiles and smiles as Arturo and I take her hands and lead her to an old recliner. He has draped the chair with a beautiful black-fringed Spanish shawl. He puts a little red cushion under her feet. She sits like a queen on a throne while he pours some green tea into a tiny porcelain cup for her.

We sit at her feet, and he serves us food in little dishes I know he has bought at the dime store (I've seen them there, but they don't look as pretty on the shelf as they do here). The china is painted with different curling designs, maybe Japanese writing. He has gone to a lot of trouble for this party.

When we finish the meal, he brings out a fluffy-looking

cake with a question mark birthday candle on it. Doña Clara laughs.

"Do we sing 'Happy Birthday to You'?" I ask, forgetting that mimes don't sing. But Arturo rises and makes gestures like a chorus director, letting me know that I should sing. I surprise myself by getting into this simple song—adding musical flourishes here and there. His mother applauds and kisses me on both cheeks.

"*Muy bien*, Doris. You sing like an angel," she says, getting up from her chair. "I'm going to go watch my *telenovela* in bed now. I'll take some of this good food with me. It's been a long day. And a happy one, thanks to you both. I'm leaving you two to clean up after this wonderful fiesta." Arturo mouths "happy birthday" to her and waves goodbye. She laughs aloud this time. I have not seen her laughing like this since before her first husband, Arturo's real dad, died. He had been a sweet man. Was laughter in the house something that Arturo's stepfather hadn't liked either? Too bad Doña Clara had picked a real loser when she married that man. Arturo returns from the kitchen and silently picks up the dishes after he signals me to stay put. He doesn't like anyone messing up his arrangements. That suits me just fine, since at home I end up picking up after Papi and Mami all the time. Suddenly thoughts of my mother fill my head and the tears start flowing. Without warning, my chest starts hurting, and soon I am bawling like a baby, right there in front of Arturo. He hands me a fancy embroidered linen napkin (Salvation Army treasures again), and watches me make a fool of myself.

I blow my nose on the napkin and try hard to rearrange my face. But the harder I try, the more the floodgates open. Arturo sits next to me, patting my hand until I get myself together.

It's nice that he isn't talking. I really don't want any words right now. That's why the pigeons are such good company. The most they ever ask is "Who? Who?" And in my mind I always answer, "Nobody, nobody, nobody." The thought makes me smile, and that dries up the overflow.

"Wanna go up to the roof?" I ask him. I think the birds must already be back—it is late, dinnertime, and twilight is over.

As we climb up the stairs, I identify my neighbors' dinners by the smells in each hallway: mainly rice and beans, *tostones*, spicy fried chicken. Man, these women have no imagination in their cooking; my mother liked to surprise us with breakfast for dinner, spaghetti for breakfast, whatever she was in the mood for. Sometimes it was irritating and even embarrassing to have friends over and get up to a morning meal of leftover party foods she had brought home from the previous night's gig. Birthday cake for breakfast is hard to explain to your friends, although no one has ever complained, and even I have to admit it's extra good with *café con leche*—an instant sugar high.

We find Doña Iris in her lounge chair. The pigeons are in their "condo." She calls us over. She looks like she wants to talk. But I really do not feel like listening to one of her long monologues. Arturo looks enthusiastic, though. His big smile slices his little face right in half. I guess mimes have to exaggerate everything. Just like Puerto Ricans.

"*¡Hijos!* Come here, look what Martha brought back," Doña Iris says. She holds up a dirty piece of gold foil, acting as if it were a diamond ring. Too bad Don Pichón is dead, or he'd be jumping up and down with excitement. (Okay, I'm exaggerating, he was too decrepit to jump, but he would have been begging her for a story about the "gold" Martha had brought him from the world.)

"She is still bringing him gifts. Juan Pablo, I mean." Doña Iris waves at the birds, now settling into their individual roosting places. "But they all know that he's gone. Did I tell you what they did on the day his spirit took flight?"

Arturo shakes his head no. The liar. We had all heard the story a dozen times, each new version of the "famous" day when the birds told Doña Iris that Don Pichón's "spirit had taken flight." The tale gets longer and more complicated each time she tells it.

When Doña Iris takes on the role of the "prophet" of El Building, she speaks in that dramatic way you only hear in church or in a play, like when she brings up this "flight of the spirit" business. Now, she takes a deep breath. She looks up at the sky. Soon she will start to intone her story. Arturo sits on the sack of bird feed, which he scoots over to be nearer to her, and I have no choice but to settle down on a box of crushed gravel, not the choicest seat. My bony bottom starts to hurt immediately. But the pain is nothing to that of listening to this *cuento*, tall tale, yet again.

"It was his eighty-fourth birthday," Doña Iris begins, reciting it like a memorized poem. "I had been baking him a chocolate cake when I heard a loud thump. I ran into my living room and saw Martha beating the glass with her beak, her wings flapping as if to tell me, *Hurry, hurry.* I knew something was wrong. I opened the window and Martha flew into my apartment. I couldn't believe it. She had never done that before, although I open my window for air every night. You know how hot these apartments get. I've thought of getting a small air conditioner, but I can't afford the electric bills . . ." I shift in my seat, stifling a yawn as she loses track of her pigeon story, hoping it's over. But Arturo taps her on the knee and nods encouragingly, which apparently jiggles her memory. I don't know whether to be grateful to him or not.

She clears her throat and continues: "Martha flew around the room as if to say, *Follow me, Iris.* My heart was about to burst. *Hijos*, I knew *la tragedia, la muerte*, was visiting us that day."

Doña Iris sighs deeply and closes her eyes like a bad actress in a bad movie. *La tragedia* is about to be replayed, and she needs to get in character. I know all her faces, since she was my babysitter for all those years. Back then it had been fun to hear her endless stories for the first time, and to watch her transform herself into different characters, sort of like watching a play, but by now it's too many encores already.

She gets up from the lawn chair, it creaks, her bones crack. She walks to the pigeon condo and rests her head on it. For a minute I think she's crying. But when she turns around, her eyes are dry.

"I found Juan Pablo here with his birds. They were all sitting on their perches guarding him like angels. Martha was at the gate here. He looked like he was alive, *hijos*, but I knew better. His spirit had taken flight and his birds were watching his earthly body until I found him."

Doña Iris comes back to her lawn chair, both she and it creaking and cracking until she finally settles down in it. I take that as my cue to get up and grab Arturo. I am getting depressed by her talk of death.

"It's late and we have to feed the pigeons now, Doña Iris," I say, pulling Arturo up from his seat. I get a canful of feed and go into the cage by myself. You are never supposed to bring in visitors at feeding time. Pigeons don't like their routines disturbed. I notice that Martha is sitting in her compartment, not leaving it even to eat. There are probably eggs under her. It'd be the first hatchlings since Don Pichón died. Only he knew how to keep the eggs from being broken when jealous males fought over the nests. It's the male birds that make trouble. Doña Iris had read that chapter in the manual aloud once, laughing at Don Pichón when he had taken the words personally. He didn't like his birds insulted in any way. He had thought she was calling them jealous machos.

When I come back out, Doña Iris has left. I feel a little bit guilty about rushing to get away from her. She's just a lonely old lady. Not much to do without me to babysit and Don Pichón to talk to. It seems like everyone I know has lost someone. We are all trying to fill the gaps in our own ways.

Doña Iris tells her stories to anyone who'll listen. But I have the feeling that no one will ever like them as much as Don Pichón had. They were her gifts to him, and his love of them was his gift to her.

Arturo is doing his tai chi. Looking good. Very focused. That's Arturo. I gaze out over the city, just beginning to blink on its lights. I think of my mother in her sparkly dress that caught the stage lights and reflected them back to us in colors. She had left that dress in her closet, taking only her newest costumes, leaving behind all the ones I had seen her wear while I was growing up. They fit me perfectly. Well, maybe not perfectly. They're a little saggy in the chest, but, after all, that's why the gel-filled bra was invented.

Before I lock the cages, I telepathically ask Martha to look for my mother and bring me a sign when she finds her. I just want to know where she is, that's all.

"Who?" Martha asks. "Who?"

"Never mind," I say.

Arturo does two cartwheels toward the door, stands at attention, waves goodbye, and leaves me to lock up the birds for the night by myself. The birds are huddling together and making soft, comforting sounds—they know they are home.

5

It is late afternoon and I sit at the kitchen table in my mother's robe, reading a library book on ESP and clairvoyance. I fail all the tests they have in the appendix. The thick velour of the robe has made me hot and itchy, and the perfume I sprayed all over gives me a throbbing headache. Maybe I am a *large* idiot instead of a medium. I take the robe off. I'm wearing her Chinese silk pajamas underneath.

I open the windows and settle down to watch a nature show on television. I can usually get into these killer-bee and warrior-ant documentaries—you can learn some useful stuff about survival from the insect world. But I can't stop thinking about my mother. Where is she? Does she worry about me?

My father comes in, all dressed up in his best suit, and puts a pizza box on the coffee table in front of me. The box is the size of the table itself. He's dressed like a window dummy, cuff links and all. Who wears cuff links anymore? He smells of a new cologne. Musk or something like Geraldo wears. Ugh.

"Going out again?" I ask as casually as I can manage.

"Margarita is cooking a special meal for me tonight before we perform at the Caribbean Moon, so I brought you this pizza. I thought you'd enjoy eating a hot meal. It's called the 'kitchen sink.'" He waits for me to smile. I don't. "It's got everything on it," he explains, in case I didn't get the joke. He has a funny, pleading look on his face. The kind that says, *Please be nice and don't ask any more questions.*

I flip the lid, and there it is: a pizza you can either eat or use as an area rug.

"I hope you and"—I pretend I've forgotten the new singer's name—"your friend have a good time."

He makes as if to go, takes a couple of steps, turns back. He looks so worried. I can tell he wants me to make it all be okay, to tell him it's fine that he prefers seeing this woman to staying home with his only child.

"Papi." I am going to say something nice, like *Say hello to Margarita.* But I stop when he turns back around and places an envelope on the table.

"It's from your mother." So this is what he has been working up to, and why he wants to get away as soon as possible. Papi has never been good at dealing with a crisis.

I let the letter lie on the table for a few moments. I place my hand on the envelope and know as sure as I've known anything in my life that my mother is not coming back, not to us anyway, not to stay. And I know I don't have any *facultades* after all. It's all a joke. I have no gift. It's all been right there for anyone to see. My mother ran off with a man. She is out there trying to become famous and to lead the glamorous life she didn't have with us. I don't need a special gift to know this.

Both of us have our eyes fixed on the letter like moths drawn to a candle.

"From Mami," I say, just to say something.

He nods. I know he wants to get this scene over with as soon as possible.

"Read it aloud, Doris?" My father puts the letter in my hand.

"*'Querida hija, querido esposo,'*" I begin reading. The letter is in Spanish. Written English was the language of school for Mami—Spanish was the language she used to express herself, like in her singing. And my Spanish is not so good, since I learned it from reading *La Prensa* to Doña Iris. She taught me Spanish as insurance for her, she said, for when her eyes got bad. It's come in handy for me, too, on a few occasions, like when I read my parents' love letters, which I "accidentally" found in a cigar box when I was looking for other stuff.

The letter says that she is at her mother's house in Puerto Rico and has been there the whole time she's been gone. She had asked Papi not to tell me until she knew for sure what she wanted to do. *Over two months.*

"'After I found out I fainted at the Sandinsky wedding because my heart needs major repairs, I decided to come home to my mother's house and think about what to do. It is a warning, this illness, that I have to fulfill my life's dream of being the best singer I can be now, or I may not get an-other chance. Doris, my beloved daughter, please understand what I am about to tell you. Your father, I think, finally does. He has always known that I have a dream to see how far my gift will take me. I want to sing different songs for different people. I need to see if my music can be understood and ap-preciated outside our little barrio. Doris, it is not that you are not an important part of my life. You are, you have always been. But I cannot wait any longer for my destiny. Soon I may be too sick or too tired to travel, or even to sing. Do you understand?' "

I stop to let myself absorb the words. Is she really sick, or is this her way of excusing her actions? Could I have been wrong all along? Was my so-called gift of looking into people's heads just more crap I picked up from hanging around Doña Iris? Papi is watching me intently, obviously expect-ing me to break down any time. But I take a deep breath and keep reading in my slow Spanish.

" 'It is not that I am abandoning you. I have watched you mature this last year and I know that you are wearing the colors of your independence. Doris, you are so talented. Do not let anyone tell you otherwise. My darling, you have a gift, too, but it isn't the one you think. Yes, you can see into the hearts and minds of people, but it's because you are a sensitive person, an artist like me, not a magician or a me-dium.' "

Papi looks at me as if he wants an explanation about my "gift," but I go on reading Mami's letter. I already know what the final message is going to be. I don't have to see into the future to know a goodbye when I hear one.

" 'Doris, there is something wrong with my heart, and I must take care of myself. My mother says that it runs in my father's family. At some point our hearts begin to beat in a different rhythm, and that is our clue to hurry and do what we need to do. It makes us hungry for life. Our blood speeds up and it is a signal that time is running out. You will say that I am being "Puerto Rican crazy," Doris. I know that the wild pumping of my heart is a medical condition. But in time you will see that we all feel this hunger to fly as far as we can.

" 'Doris, I did not mean to worry you. I just needed a little time to decide what to do after I got my diagnosis. I had to get second opinions to make sure there was no mistake, and to make sure I understood it all clearly, so I could explain it to you. Your father has known where and how to find me if you had really needed me, Doris. I asked him to wait until I had all the facts. The doctors say that I may have many good years to live if I take care of myself.

" 'I will not be away from you for all the time that I have left, but I am going to take some time for my music. Your grandmother will take care of me when I need it. She is giving me this as a gift. Doris, I can only hope to live long enough to give you such a gift someday. Please, be happy for me. Both of you be happy and don't forget that I love you.' "

The letter goes on for several more paragraphs. It gives us a description of her life now, one line about Geraldo helping her make new connections: voice lessons at the university, a gig in a nightclub where he knows important people. She tells us the titles of the songs she is now singing: "Sabor a Mí," "Lágrimas Negras," "Ojos Negros," "Cielito Lindo." A professor has arranged for her to sing with a combo made up of university students and musicians who tour the island on weekends. Their goal is to preserve the traditional music of the island. They perform in parks, schools, and retirement homes. She sings the old songs in Spanish. She says Geraldo thinks the exposure is a good jump start to her career on the island, but he's anxious to start making real money. And yes, she is getting medical treatment. Perhaps I will come see her this summer? She hopes we can sing together again. She calls me her *cielito lindo*, after the title of the old song she sang to me when she rocked me to sleep; I think it means "my child from heaven," or something like that. The letter closes with *besos y abrazos*, kisses and hugs. And a P.S.: "Your *papi* will be okay, Doris. He and I have talked. I know about the new singer. She's a good person. By now you know that you can take care of yourself. This is not a tragedy. Your father and I already know that we no longer belong together. A man and a woman are not bound by blood as a mother and her child are. He will always be your father and I will always be your mother, but we will be a family in a different way."

I fold the pages and hand them across the table. My father's been crying silently as I read the letter.

He lightly touches his fingers to mine. "Do you understand, Doris? All of it?"

"Yes." I understand well enough. But I am not really sure I understand why *I* am not part of my mother's flight plan. I wouldn't have held her back. I feel anger and relief all at once. At least *she's* got her mother to take care of her, even if I don't have mine.

"It will be okay." My father is patting my shoulder and avoiding my eyes. "She needs time on her own. Your *abuela* will take good care of her. We'll be okay, too."

I have nothing to say. I just want to be alone and think this over. Obviously, I have been proven a fake medium. The only thing I had been right about was the feeling I had from the start that she wasn't coming back. But I had not believed she was really sick.

I feel sad, yes, yet somehow also free. It's like when there is an emergency and everyone is running around not knowing what to do, and then someone says, "This is what's happening, and this is what you can do." My mother is gone from our lives, for now, maybe forever. In a way, I am glad to know the bad news. It is a release from the agony of suspense. The letter is a declaration of her own independence. And of mine.

"Doris?"

My father's face is by now tear-streaked. I can tell he is ready for a heart-to-heart talk about all the complicated stuff that I'll have to start dealing with soon, like her illness, and why he did not tell me where she was. I suspect it's because they think that the less I know, the less I'll suffer. But they are wrong. It is better to know the truth, even if at first it feels like a punishment I don't deserve.

But before I ask my father about anything, I want to try to answer some questions for myself.

"Doris, will you come see the new show at the Caribbean Moon tonight?" my father asks me. "My set starts at ten. I could come get you. I don't want you to be alone right now."

"No, thank you. I have plans." I don't, really, but I am ready to make some. If I'm going to have a new life, it has to start right now. And the Caribbean Moon and ¡Caliente! ¡Caliente!, even with the new singer, is old news to me.

He acts like he's disappointed, but I know he wants his night out with his girlfriend. Or maybe he expected tears from me, like in any good old *telenovela*. Women are always drowning in their own tears. Really, one thing about us Latinos—we have to have our *tragedias*.

"Want some cold pizza?" I ask him, cool as anything. I open the huge box between us and peek around it, smiling as if it were just any old day. He gets up, sighs, and, looking sort of hurt and scared, as if I had turned into a wicked witch just like Mami on one of her bad days, he leaves the apartment.

I am *furious*. Both my parents seem to find it so easy to destroy my life and then act as if they are doing nothing. They talk it over, decide that they want to go their separate ways, and then generously let me know their plans when it's too late to give them my take on the situation. Kids don't often get speaking parts in the movie of their parents' lives. They are the extras in their family feature presentations. They can cut you out of the movie any time it suits them. Okay.

Fine with me. From this moment on, I decide to reinvent Doris in my own image, not theirs.

That evening, as I race up the stairs to watch the pigeons flying home, and to think about what I can do to celebrate my newly declared independence, I run into Arturo. He tells me right away that he is not a mime anymore. He misses talking on the telephone. I am a little disappointed.

"Guess what?" he says. "My stepfather finally called. My mother told him she had had enough of his abuse and that she is going to have the locks changed in our apartment. They're getting a divorce, Doris." Arturo does a little salsa step on the landing when he tells me this.

"We're really free, free of the Macho Monster. Let's have a party . . ."

He does not shut up until we get to the roof. Then I tell him to please zip it up for a while. Pigeons are very nervous birds.

Martha's flight home is beautiful. The sun is setting at her back as she swoops down for a landing. She is like a dancer bathed in a gold spotlight. Her wings become white fans as they open wide. It's like she's showing us the evening sky and the city below. The sunset is a stage for her, where footlights are just beginning to light up. I point her dance out to Arturo, who immediately begins imitating her in a rooftop ballet of his own. Martha lands on the ledge. Her balance is perfect.

"Looks like she's got a worm in her mouth," Arturo observes, making a disgusted face.

"No, son, it's not a *gusano* Martha brings us. It's news of the world."

Arturo and I jump into each other's arms at the unexpected sound of Doña Iris's voice behind us. She has been there all along, piled like a bundle of gray rags in her folding chair. In the twilight, she's hard to see.

Doña Iris joins us and takes the dirty piece of glossy paper with gold letters from the bird's beak. I notice that she holds Martha correctly, cupping her wings with one hand, just like the manual says you ought to hold a bird.

"Uh-huh." She nods her head, squinting at the scrap of paper. Arturo and I look at each other—apparently the old woman has finally lost it.

"Look, children, it is a message for one of us. It does not pertain to me. Come see if it's for you."

Arturo takes the piece of dirty paper first. He shrugs his shoulders. I grab it from him and read: " 'You will soon . . .' " It is a torn piece of a horoscope column. I shrug my shoulders, too. I am tired of trying to see into the future. Starting right now, I plan to live for today. I let the scrap fall over the ledge. The wind carries it to another roof. Both Doña Iris and Arturo look at me like I've tossed away a hundred-dollar bill.

I start to fill bowls with bird chow. The old lady follows me. Bad move. Birds don't like their routines changed.

"It is time to lock the birds up for the night, Doris. Come, before it is too dark to see."

I let Doña Iris tell me what to do, although I have done it a hundred times before. She likes quoting from the

Manual of Pigeon Breeding, Care, and Feeding that she carries in her pocket. It had belonged to Don Pichón, who brought it home after the war. The book is falling apart, held together with a rubber band.

"The hatchlings are called squabs," she informs me while reaching under a roosting bird, who protests loudly. She doesn't take the hint.

"That's good to know." I look in every condo unit to make sure all the birds are in for the night.

Martha is the first to settle in. She squats gently down on her eggs. Pigeons sit on their eggs in shifts and it is her turn. She tucks her beak inside her wing as if her day's flight had exhausted her. Her eyes close immediately. I wonder if birds dream when they sleep. And if they do dream, do they dream of flying, and of the places they've seen?

Part Two

As soon as a young pigeon is capable of feeling the same (apparent) specific emotional moods as the adult it will "try" to utter the adult calls.

6

It's like this. One day I am one person, Doris, someone's daughter, someone's friend, neither beautiful nor hideously ugly, not a dimwit, and not a genius, just good old Doris, and then I am suddenly *that poor girl* to my friends, teachers, and neighbors—the pitiful daughter of a runaway mother.

I am managing to stay in school for the year, although my grades are shot. Last term I had straight A's. Everybody understands that it is a difficult time for *la pobre* Doris, whose mother has abandoned the family. The teachers are acting in an unnatural, maternal way toward me, and telling my classmates to be kind to me. I'm getting pretty sick of being treated like a dearly beloved at my own funeral, tired of my so-called friends "letting me have some space."

Even my outrageous clothes don't get a reaction anymore. I guess everyone thinks I'm acting out my anger. I mean, it's like everyone goes home to watch the talk shows about troubled kids and dysfunctional families and then they practice their theories on me: Let her come to you when she's ready. Give her some space. Don't crowd her in. Be patient with her during her crisis. Tolerate some displays of rebellion; they'll help her vent. I feel like a walking advertisement for a show: *Your Disturbed Teen and How to Cope.*

What they don't know is that I'm okay with my mother leaving. In fact, I'm glad to have her finally do something instead of complaining all the time about her talent going to waste. She's called to say everything is great on the island. She's happy singing with the combo and loves the gigs they are doing. She claims her medicines are helping her heart condition. For some reason the doctor decided not to operate right now. She also wants to know how I'm doing. I don't say much. I don't tell her that when I stopped having my dreams about her, I started having a life. That's the real change for me.

It may seem like my mother's leaving would have serious consequences. But, for us, it's as if we've been riding in two cars and she's taken a different exit ramp. Before she left, we were not exactly the *normal* American family, but we were a family. Now it's just me and my father, who used to be her husband and my *papi*, but not anymore. His new girlfriend calls him "Papi," so I try not to call him anything.

I am nobody's concern now. I am the new Doris, the one who takes care of herself first. Things are changing fast. But they don't change in some ways. Money is still left for me on the table, sometimes with an emergency number to call. My father still comes home to change his clothes, and then dashes out again, busier than ever managing his two bands.

But now, he is spending any extra time he has with Margarita. Sometimes he brings her home. Tonight I went into the living room expecting to watch TV by myself, but I discovered him cuddled up with her on the sofa. She's a full head taller than he is, and has twenty pounds or more on him, too. It takes some doing to fit themselves into a loving pretzel. *Ugh.*

"How was school today, Doris?" he asks, pretending to be interested in me, although his hands are all over her, and that's a lot of territory to cover.

"School's closed on Saturdays."

"Is that a new rule?" He laughs.

Margarita giggles as if he is real funny.

"So what have you been doing with yourself today?"

"Hanging."

"Hanging out with the birds?" Margarita flashes me one of her stage smiles, both upper and lower teeth bared.

I decide to pretend I didn't hear the question.

On the television a blond actor and a blond actress are going at it. My father leans his face over Margarita's, and hers goes soft. I slam the door as I leave.

I go by Arturo's, but he's out. His mother is alone, watching the Spanish shopping channel. She doesn't know when he'll be home. Arturo is the phantom of the night, often wandering the streets alone. This habit may have started when his home life became a nightmare, or even before, since he's always been a loner. I just know that around sunset Arturo often gets an urge to walk the city. It used to drive his mother crazy. You could hear the creaking window of her apartment pushed open at some point during the night. She'd stick her head out no matter how cold it was and call out his name. He told me that this humiliated him, being called in like a baby. Especially since you could also hear his stepfather calling him names and cursing him out. I think his mother finally realized that Arturo wasn't out getting into trouble, but getting away from it. Now they seem to have things worked out. She doesn't worry, and he's usually in by midnight.

I decide to try to see my friend Yolanda, who also lives in our building. My mother had told me I couldn't hang out with her after Yoli got arrested for shoplifting. But Yoli's not a criminal; she's just trying to have a little fun. Besides, since her old man got killed during a robbery at the store where he'd been a security guard, she's been a real rebel. She is almost failing school. And she acts like she doesn't care what anybody thinks. I'd been the only one who really understood her, and I dropped her months ago. It had been one of Mami's ultimatums: "Either you stay away from that trashy Yolanda, or I'll side with your father about sending you to Catholic school." I confess that at the time I was beginning to like Central High, so it wasn't hard to let my friendship with Yolanda slide. I had gotten into my classes, and found out I liked reading. But mainly, I had my eye on a boy named Danny. So after a while I just stopped seeing Yolanda. Anyone else, and she would have gotten revenge—Yoli is an eye-for-an-eye sort of person. But I knew she'd give me a second chance. After all, I have the "abandoned child" label on my side now, and, besides, she doesn't exactly have a whole bunch of friends.

Still, instead of risking personal contact right away, I go outside and call her from a pay phone on the street in case her mother is sleeping, or in the event that she wants to curse me out. At least I'll have a chance to escape. But she invites me up as if nothing has happened between us. I see right away that she has a black eye. Kenny hit her, she tells me, sounding almost proud. They go at each other, she tells me, because they are passionate people. She told me before that she likes getting into all-out rowdy fights with Kenny, then making up. I had always assumed she was exaggerating.

"I broke up with Kenny," she tells me, "but it's not because of the black eye. I'll tell you more about it later."

I can't wait to hear what Kenny has done that has made Yolanda mad. It has to be something serious, like stealing a Corvette and forgetting to take her somewhere nice in it. Yolanda has a high tolerance for Kenny's criminal activity.

Yolanda grabs my arm and rubs her head on mine, acting as if she had just seen me yesterday. We head downtown. It feels good to be walking with my friend again.

We pass by the big clock at the bank. Eleven-thirty. It's late, at least for me. It used to be that I was out after midnight only when my parents brought me to some dim nightclub where they had a gig. Usually I wound up sleeping in a booth, so I never cared much for the late-night hours. But tonight feels different.

For some unknown reason, Yolanda hugs me hard as we wait for the light to change. It's what I've always liked about my friendship with this girl. She can hate me one minute, and the next she'll have her arms around me like I'm her last friend on earth. Some men in a car pull up to the light and yell out some crass words at us. She gives them the finger. They slow down and I start to pull Yolanda back. She runs toward their windshield brandishing her father's old security-guard nightstick. The car starts to back up, reversing right in the middle of the street. We see that there are three men with beer cans in their hands, all of them obviously drunk, and angry at us. After her show, Yolanda grabs my hand and we run. Brakes squeal—we duck into the alley between the bodega and the music shop. It's dark and smells like a public toilet, but it goes all the way through to the other side of the block.

"Come on, Yoli." I grab her hand and we run as fast as we can—giggling—down the alley. But suddenly I hear a voice I think I recognize. There are other sounds, too. Like hitting and kicking, and also like someone grunting as if in pain. It's coming from behind a dumpster.

Yolanda and I stand frozen.

"Doris! What's that?" Yolanda whispers in my ear. She grabs my hand, looking one way, then the other. Even in the dark, I can see how bright her eyes are. She loves this kind of predicament. I understand her question. We have a choice. We can run past the mugging, which is obviously what's going on behind the dumpster, or we can run back to the street where the three amigos in the car may still be waiting for us.

"Let's call the cops." My thought is to run to the pay phone on the other side of the dumpster and dial 911. Yolanda shakes her head no. The scuffling noises have ended. But we hear crying. We flatten ourselves on the wall as two guys in black, stocking masks and all, run past us. We hear moaning and noises like somebody is struggling.

"Come on, Yolanda, let's go call the police." I am scared now. What if someone is dying back there? We'll be witnesses to a murder. I admit that I had wanted a little excitement, but not this much.

But Yolanda is already following the cries coming from behind the dumpster.

"Doris!" I hear something in her voice and have a hunch that I'm in for a terrible surprise.

I run toward her. She's kneeling on the ground, leaning over a body. I can see legs and a bloody hand.

I kneel next to Yolanda and look at the face she is cradling in her arms.

"¡Dios mio! What happened to you?"

Arturo turns his bruised and bloody face away from me. Yolanda points to the side of the dumpster. Arturo's name is scrawled with an X, and over it, the shark's jaw symbol of the Tiburones gang.

"It must be a bash night in our happy little city," Yolanda says, wrapping her neck scarf around Arturo's head. I'm too stunned to say anything. I have questions of my own, but I can see that we need to get him home or to the hospital.

"Should I call the police?" I ask. Yolanda has stopped the bleeding as best she can, and is now helping Arturo sit up against the wall.

"No, Doris. Call my mother." Arturo grabs my hand. "Tell her what happened so she won't be frightened when she sees me."

"But, Arturo, you might need stitches."

"Do what he says, Doris." Yolanda has a strange glazed look in her eyes. With her black eye, blood on her clothes, and Arturo leaning against her, she looks like a refugee from a war.

I run out of the alley and toward the streetlight. The guys in the car are gone. The street is practically deserted. I walk to the pay phone to call Arturo's mother and then go back and help Yolanda get Arturo on his feet.

Arturo walks painfully between us. I put my arm around his waist. He feels so bony, like a bird does when you slide your fingers under its feathers to look for ticks. I can feel his rib cage through his blood-soaked shirt. Yolanda is strangely silent. Her eyes are big and bright like she's holding back tears.

Arturo's mother wraps her arms around her son as soon as we come in, and helps him into his room.

Yolanda and I sit, not looking at each other, in the room that Arturo painted and decorated in bright colors for his mother's birthday party: sky blue walls, sheer curtains draped around the four walls like banks of puffy clouds, an old cocktail table painted bright yellow and shellacked, and the purple rug that has seen better days. I let my eyes go from color to color and shape to shape. It's like being inside a rainbow.

"It's amazing what Arturo can do with a little paint and some junk," I say to Yolanda, hoping to bring her out of her daze. I am surprised that her mood has changed so drastically, from excitement to this sort of weird trance.

I notice that Arturo's easel is by the window. I go take a closer look. He's working on a charcoal drawing of a pigeon with a scrap of ribbon in its beak.

"It's Martha."

But Yolanda doesn't respond. Arturo's mother comes out of the room with some bloody towels in her hands.

"*Niñas*, thank you for bringing my son home. I believe that he will be fine. I will take him to the emergency clinic in a few hours if he isn't better." She looks so sad again. I want her to be my mother. I could have been killed out there tonight, and my mother wouldn't even know it. She is probably dancing with Geraldo under the Caribbean moon. I feel nauseated at the thought.

I look at the clock then. It's three in the morning! I can only hope my father is still being distracted by his girlfriend and hasn't noticed that I'm not home.

"Señora." I'm startled by Yolanda's grim tone, and by her politeness. "May I speak with Arturo for a few minutes?"

"I don't think it is a good idea, *hija*."

"Please, señora, it's very important. It's about the ones who did this to him."

"You know who did this?" I'm the one who asks. Arturo's mother is already leading Yolanda to his room.

Afterward, Yolanda doesn't answer my questions. She insists that we go into her apartment before I go up to mine. Her mother will not be home until morning.

"I know one of them was Kenny, Doris."

"How do you know? I mean, they were wearing masks. Yolanda, just because you're mad at Kenny, you can't accuse someone of a crime . . ."

Yolanda laughs sarcastically. "It was Kenny. I know every inch of that guy. I *know* him, *chica*. I know his moves. It was Kenny. He's got a problem with Arturo. Always has."

"What about the other guy?"

"Don't know. I know our boy Kenny, though." Suddenly she looks exhausted. She's different from the way I remember her, even from a few months ago. Her face seems older now, and her voice has an edge. But there is something about her, a sort of anger, that is even scarier to me, something Doña Iris had pointed out when I had taken Yolanda up to the roof in the past.

"That *niña* is carrying unhappiness around inside her like a bomb waiting to explode. Do you see how her presence frightens the birds? They can feel that she is *peligrosa*. Danger. Walking danger."

I had laughed about this with Yolanda after Doña Iris had

left us alone on the roof. The old woman had been nervous like a scared bird herself when Yoli was around, as if she expected Yolanda to do something crazy. I knew Yolanda felt offended by Doña Iris's obvious distrust of her.

One day, Yolanda had even leaned way over the edge of the roof and yelled, "I am dangerous. I am *peligrosa*. Look out, world!" We had made a game of it and a secret joke. Whenever she passed me notes in school, she signed them La Peligrosa. Declaring herself the Dangerous One.

But now it all feels different. Maybe it's the lateness of the hour, or the sight of my gentle friend Arturo hurt and bleeding, and the two of us in our bloody clothes talking in whispers even though there's no one to hear us—but it all adds up to a feeling of impending doom. Suddenly I wish I were safe in my bed, with Mami and Papi in the next room—just a whisper away.

"I think Kenny has gone too far, Doris. He's no good."

"Yolanda, you're wrong. I know Kenny has always been mean to Arturo, but I don't think he would attack him. Hey, we all went to grammar school together, remember?"

"Doris, you *are* clueless." Yolanda's voice turns harsh. I can tell she thinks I'm a wimp. I start to get up from her mother's couch, which, I notice, we have stained with Arturo's blood, but she yanks me back down.

"You've been out of touch, my friend, wrapped up in your own problems. We all know about your mom's *big escape*." Yolanda speaks right into my face. Her eyes are filled with tears, but she is not letting them fall. I try to pry her hand from my arm. She continues digging her nails into me and it hurts.

"I have to go, Yolanda, or my father will have a fit. I'll call you tomorrow."

"Listen, Doris. You stopped being my friend months ago, so you don't know what's been happening in my life. You still don't know why I broke up with Kenny."

"Because he's a jerk who's always stoned. That's why. I know all I need to know about your boyfriend. I mean, *ex*-boyfriend." I was tired of hearing about Kenny. I was worried about Arturo.

"That's kid stuff. I was pretty lonely after you abandoned me, Doris. I'm not exactly popular in this barrio, you know. It's that rep as La Peligrosa the witch laid on me." She tries to make it a joke, but her eyes, full of sadness, betray her.

"I'm sorry, Yolanda." And I really am. I never knew Yolanda depended on my friendship so much. She didn't act like it. She never called me.

"You might have to prove it to me, Doris. I don't really believe you are sorry."

"Yolanda, not tonight. Please, can we talk about this to-morrow?"

"You can leave as soon as I tell you something. It's a secret that you can't tell anyone. Just like old times, remember? It has to do with Kenny. But first I want to show you some-thing." She goes into her room and comes out with a small wooden box. It says DOMINOES in block letters on top.

"Look what I found. It was my father's."

"His *dominoes*?" I have a zoned-out moment. Is Yolanda going to demand that I play a game of dominoes with her before she lets me go home? It'd make a great opening shot for a movie scene: two teenage girls in bloody clothes are playing dominoes at four a.m. Close-up of the one in combat boots: her pupils are glowing red, and she is about to reveal that she is not just another wild Latina, she is the alien creature known as the *chupacabras*. The alien vampire that sucks the blood out of goats and cattle on the island has now moved to an American barrio and taken the shape of a girl. Close-up of the other girl in jeans and a rhinestone-studded top. She is wild-eyed and obviously scared. What a nightmare. I need to go home, take a bath, sleep. I need to get this night over with.

But Yolanda's dead set on telling me her secret. I keep thinking about how I'll manage to get into my apartment without waking my father. But I have a strong feeling that Yoli has to talk or she'll explode. In my mind, I hear Doña Iris's words about this girl, and this time they spook me: "Like a bomb waiting to explode."

Yolanda opens the box and pulls it out. It's silver with a black handle. She holds it in the palm of her hand and it glints in the dim light from the streetlamp.

"It was my father's revolver. He had it in his hand the day he was killed."

"Why do you have it?"

"It belongs to my mother, but she put it in a drawer and forgot about it. I know he wouldn't mind if I took it."

"Is it loaded?"

"No, the bullets are in her jewelry box. I saw three of them when I borrowed her earrings the other day."

It feels strangely right to be ending this night admiring a silver gun. I turn it over in my hands. It's cool to the touch, heavier than it looks. This seems to satisfy Yolanda. I am tired beyond words. I feel like I'm moving underwater and hear everything as if from far away. Yolanda can probably talk me into just about anything at this point. She has delivered on the adrenaline charge I had been hoping for earlier. Now I'm sliding down into a zombie state.

"Well, just as long as you don't shoot anybody with it." I hand the gun back to her. I try to act casual so that maybe she'll see that I am not that impressed with it, and will finally let me go home.

"La Peligrosa makes no promises." She puts the gun back in the box. "Now I will tell you my secret."

I sigh deeply and sit back one more time. I hope that Yoli is not going to confess to holding up a store with the gun, or anything else I'd have to carry around like my own unexploded bomb.

Again she surprises me, taking my hand in hers. "Doris, remember that week when practically everyone at school was sick with the flu? When I stayed out 'sick' too? But I didn't have the flu. Doris, I had a miscarriage. It was Kenny's baby."

I feel my jaw drop. My eyes go wide even though I want to sleep more than anything else in the world. Yolanda stares at me, makes a face, and starts laughing out loud, almost hysterically.

"You look so funny, Doris." She points at me and howls with laughter. I pull away from her hand, still clamped down on mine, and run for the door.

"Doris!" I look back when I hear Yolanda call out my name in a strange, sort of strangled voice. She begins sobbing as if her harsh laughter had broken a dam holding back the tears. She curls up in her mother's sofa, crying like a baby herself.

But I can't turn back. I am so tired. I feel I have just enough strength to climb the stairs to my apartment.

I shut the door to Yolanda's apartment quietly behind me. My life of independence has certainly had a bang-up start.

Margarita opens the door when she hears me fiddling with the lock. I am too sleepy and miserable to fit the key in the hole on the first try.

"Doris! Look at you, what happened!?" I practically fall into her arms. She's wearing my father's yellow silk pajamas. The ones that my mother had given him for his last birthday and that he never wore.

I try to get by her, but my father has appeared in the kitchen. He looks confused and angry at the same time. He is in street clothes because he's been out looking for me.

"Doris! I've been looking for you everywhere, waking up people, and going crazy with worry. Where the hell have you been? *¡Diablos!* Are you hurt?" He switches on the bright kitchen light and I am blinded for a moment. I had forgotten that I have Arturo's blood all over my jeans, my white T-shirt, and the sequined top I'd borrowed from my mother's closet.

Too tired to fight it, I let him lead me to a chair at the kitchen table. Both of them are looking at me in horror. I must be a sight. Suddenly it's like I'm in an *America's Most Wanted* episode. The interrogation scene is about to begin. I know I still have some rights, though.

"Can I have a Coke?"

"Doris! *¡Ay bendito!* You're covered in blood, it's five in the morning . . ."

"Four-forty-seven," I correct him, looking up at the Coors Beer clock on the wall. Time is an important element in crime stories. I feel an out-of-body experience coming on.

"Doris!" he yells again, but I can see that he's more frightened than angry. And he has such a pathetic look in his eyes, as if he's about to start crying. Actually, he looks as hysterical as I feel. I decide I'd better explain. Margarita has now wrapped her big arms around his shoulders and is stroking his hair. If my mother were here, she'd know that he's a grown man, for heaven's sake, and I'm the one who needs the attention. But Ms. M., the girlfriend, has no children of her own, so her priorities are, of course, screwed up. But then, where is my dear *mami* in my hour of need?

"Arturo got mugged by a gang. I got him home. It's his blood. I'm not hurt. Can I go take a bath now?"

"No! Not until you tell us where you were all night," my father demands. He starts toward me as if to grab me or something, but Margarita holds him back with a full frontal body block. I think she'd make a good female wrestler.

"We have been up all night worried sick. We even called St. Joseph's hospital. If your mother were here . . ."

"What about my mother? She's starting a new life on a tropical island. What does she care if I live or die in this ugly old barrio?" I know I'm being cruel, but I'm angry at my father. He doesn't seem to miss my mother, and she doesn't seem to miss us. I'm the one left out in the cold.

My father sits down at the kitchen table and puts his face in his hands. He is not good at conflict resolution. When it doesn't have to do with business, he's lost. Mami had always been the one who made the decisions about me, about us. I am beginning to feel a little lost myself. I mean, if the so-called grownups around you don't have answers to the big questions, who are you going to ask?

I sit there. He sits there. Finally Margarita clears her throat. Her voice is deep, and her *harrumph* startles me. My mother's voice is a high soprano, like a songbird's call next to this foghorn.

"Doris, what if I fix you a hot bath? I think you should get out of those clothes. Is your friend going to be okay? I'll make you some cocoa while you change . . ." She starts walking toward me and I'm afraid she's going to engulf me like she does him.

"I can draw my own bath. And I hate cocoa, so don't bother." I feel mean saying it, but their concern for me is too little, too late. I leave the two of them in the kitchen and lock myself in the bathroom. I take my bloody clothes off and step into the tub. I let the water rise to the top of my ears. Then I go limp and try to float.

"Anger is heavier than joy," Doña Iris had once said to me, the time I threw a tantrum when my parents had left town without me one summer. And she's right. I sink.

Okay. So maybe I do miss my mother. But I'm doing fine. Back in my room I pull the cigar box, Hav-A-Tampa, from under my bed. I had taken it from their bedroom. My father wouldn't miss it. The cigar box is where Mami kept old photos and other junk from her past. There is a picture of her as a child, singing at what looked like a talent show in Puerto Rico. She is wearing a frilly dress and ribbons in her wild hair. Her mouth is open in song and her eyes have that familiar faraway look she always gets when she's into her singing. In the background there is a sign in Spanish advertising Corona beer. Are all social events on the island sponsored by beer? It's one of those questions I meant to ask my mother. She was also a finalist in the Queen of Corona competition, and I know there was a trophy around somewhere for first place in the Miller Beer La Voz singing competition. My father certainly contributes to the beer industry's profit index, and so do most Latinos I know. I've never had a taste for it myself. In the box I find an old travel brochure for Puerto Rico, the kind that looks like the palm trees were paint-by-numbers watercolors. It lists the population (crowded little island), climate (*perfecto*), kinds of birds (illustrations of little green parrots and yellow *reinitas*, warblers of some kind), and a map of the island. It shows mountains in the middle and one main road that neatly divides it and leads straight to the town where my *abuela* lives and my mother is supposedly staying. It seems to me that my block here in the city is more complicated than that entire country! I take out the map to study later. In the bottom of the box is my birth certificate with my baby footprint. Was I ever that tiny? In a small jeweler's box I find her wedding band. So she had taken all her other jewelry, but left her wedding ring.

I close the box and put it back under my bed. I lie back. The heaviness had left me for the few minutes it took to look in her box of treasures, but now, when I think of that ring, I feel a pain in my chest that I think will stay with me for days. Anger is heavier than joy or grief.

7

On Monday, before school, I go up to check on the birds. I am late to feed them and they are restless, anxious to be on their way. They eat quickly, and when I open the cage doors they rush by me and disappear over the city. I had wanted to see them circling above in their early-morning ballet. But because of their haste to be on their way, I have been denied my few minutes of peace watching them.

In the halls of Central High there has been a lot of talk about Arturo's beating. I find him at his locker, taking out books for his next class. He has a big bandage over his left eye.

"Just a fight," I hear him tell a girl who has a reputation for being a big gossip. She is pretending concern, but she's a bad actress. She tries to touch his face, but he avoids her. "It's nothing. Just a scratch." He says his lines like an actor in a movie. He's good. I wink at him from behind her back.

"A scratch? Then you must have gotten in a cat fight!" She says this loud so that her friends can hear. She is staging a

show for them. They all laugh in a mean way. Arturo turns
his attention to me.

"My guardian angel," he says. "I have a reward for you."
From his locker, he pulls out a framed charcoal drawing of a
pigeon with a gold ribbon in its beak. It's the same one I had
seen at his house on Saturday night.

"I finished it yesterday since my mother would not let me
out of the house, even after the doctor at the emergency clinic
said I had suffered no permanent damage. She wouldn't even
let me come to the phone when you called."

I can't understand how he can be so cheerful after what
happened to him. But then I remember that Arturo would
never let on that he's hurt in front of his enemies. That's how
he's survived in the mean halls of Central. I get to see the
funny, sensitive artist; others see only what Arturo wants
them to see.

I thank him for the drawing of Martha. I hadn't seen her
that morning. Had I just missed her as they all rushed past me?
She usually leads the other birds out on their morning flight.

We walk together to our second-period class (and Arturo's
favorite), English. We see Yoli coming out of the girls' bathroom. She doesn't look good. Her face is smeared with old
mascara and lipstick. Instead of her usual outfit of trashy-
sexy tights and spandex with a Tiburones denim jacket, she
is wearing a man's shirt over baggy jeans; both are black. Her
brown roots are showing through her brassy red-dyed hair,
and she looks almost thirty years old. She passes us like she's
lost in space, barely acknowledging my hello.

"I think she's high," Arturo says. "Her pupils are gone, did you see?" I don't agree. Yolanda looks like I do when I am hurting so much I can hardly get out of bed.

"Arturo, do you know who beat you up?"

"Yes."

We are at the door to AP English. Yolanda walks like a robot past her classroom and down the hall toward the exit sign. She's not in the college prep program, but I know she has a class at the same hour as ours, business English or something.

"Yolanda thinks Kenny Matoa did it."

"She's right, Doris."

"What are you going to do about it?"

He doesn't have a chance to answer me before the teacher closes the door. Arturo just smiles in a strange way as we head toward our seats. Mr. Sanders begins taking roll.

Today we're discussing the novel *Heart of Darkness*.

"Does anyone know what final words Mr. Kurtz speaks to Marlow deep in the heart of the jungle, and what they may mean?"

" 'The horror! The horror!' " I say before I can stop myself.

"That's correct, Doris," Mr. Sanders says, "but can we raise our hands before speaking? Remember what I have said again and again to you: courtesy and a certain amount of respect for manners are essential to our coexisting as civilized people in this world."

The class laughs at this. Mr. Sanders drops in at Central like a visiting alien from his suburban home to teach us barrio and inner-city kids. He wears Dockers khaki pants and white Oxford shirts with colorful ties his wife brings back from her travels—she's a big-shot lawyer. Still, as cornball and clueless as he is, he knows his stuff, so we mostly put up with him. But his Miss Manners lectures are hard to take with a straight face after a typical weekend in the barrio. I mean, what does the man do on weekends? Water his lawn, wash his minivan, watch football with his suburban buddies? Does he get out into the *real* world? Arturo leans over to whisper: "Next time I get mugged, I am going to insist on a *please* and a *thank you* from my attackers."

"Arturo, since you are already talking, perhaps you can explicate the meaning of 'The horror! The horror!' for our benefit."

And Arturo does just that. He *explicates for our benefit* what the horror meant in Conrad's book—something about facing our own evil natures; but we know he has experienced the horror himself. All we have to do is look at his bandaged eye and bruised face to understand what it means to live in the heart of darkness.

Chorus is my favorite class. Yolanda likes it, too, which is why she came back to class for last period.

Our Mexican-American—or as she prefers ("If we *must* have labels, let them be accurate") *Chicana*—music teacher, Ms. Torres, is from L.A. (She likes to sing it out as La-La Land.) She is a real person from a real place, not that different from this city, only sunnier. She grew up in a tough barrio and nothing, *nada*, shocks her. The only thing that makes her nuts is if we don't sing right. Singing right in her class means singing in harmony and with passion. That is one of her favorite words, *passion*. She says she has a passion for music, and that's the only reason she is there teaching us. She likes to tell her classes that music saved her life, literally. She often recounts the story of the day she auditioned for the school orchestra and there was a drive-by shooting in front of her house. Her best friend was killed by a stray bullet. She would have been out in the yard with her friend and could have been shot, too, if she hadn't been waiting her turn to play the one piano her school had. After that happened, she had dedicated her life to music, and her passion is teaching kids like us to understand that music can save us, too.

She is a walking cliché—she's the girl from East L.A. who lives to do good, and to help others get away from *the horror, the horror* of a wasted life. Ms. Torres from La-La Land is intense, but she is also sincere. You can tell she really believes that she's on a mission from God, like the Blues Brothers (my father's favorite movie; we've watched it like three hundred times), to save us inner-city kids from—an unbearable life without music.

Ms. Torres also looks like you want your mother to look, kind of solid in her pantsuits, but classy and soft, too—maternal. Since I sit in front of her every day during fifth period, I've had a lot of time to watch Ms. Torres. For a whole year, I've looked into her head and seen musical notes dancing around. When she tells us about her childhood in a

California barrio, I imagine a neighborhood of little pink houses where gangsta-types lived with their worried Chicana mothers, all looking like Ms. T. When she tells us about her early life and how she reinvented herself, she likes to say that she has always "flown against the wind." And how did she do it? By having a driving passion for her art.

Even Kenny Matoa, the *alleged* mugger and Central High's resident troubled teen, behaves himself (more or less, that is, *mas o menos*) in chorus. Not that he'd be allowed to stay if he didn't. You don't just automatically get into chorus, even if you're a great singer; Ms. T. *invites* people into her Advanced Chorus class. It's her personal project, and she puts a lot of her own time, even her own money, into it. She takes us to concerts in the city when it's something she can't justify to her patron saint, the Virgin of Guadalupe, having us miss. That's how she puts it, as if God's mother were going to make her explain why she had not taken us to a violin concert by the greatest living child prodigy.

"Doris, you should train that voice," Ms. T. would tell me almost as often as my mother asked me to sing with her at weddings and parties. I kept telling them both I wasn't interested in singing. But now that Mami is gone, I find that I miss having music around the house. Sometimes I still think I hear her voice.

In chorus it's Arturo who is the star, though. He knows all the Broadway show songs and he reads music, too. So he and Ms. T. have some kind of musical rapport going. We're a small group this semester, mainly Latinos and one

African-American girl, since Ms. T. has decided to concentrate on Spanish songs for the last performance at graduation. For the first time ever, there will be as many Latino kids as white kids graduating from Central.

We've been listening to salsa and classical Mexican mariachi music as well as Tejano tunes, Caribbean music, and all kinds of ancient stuff. Any of us who want to sing a solo at the graduation ceremony have to present a song to the class, and Ms. T. will decide who gets to perform.

Today everybody is watching Arturo setting up his recorded music. He looks dramatic in a black silk shirt and black jeans, his main accessory being the huge bandage over his left eye. His right eye has a purple circle around it. I glance over at Kenny Matoa. He has bulked out this year, doing weights and probably steroids, too—there isn't a pill or drug Matoa doesn't like, or at least that's the word out on him. He's only managing to stay in school because he's an excellent wrestler—that is, when he isn't out performing criminal acts—and because he has a terrific voice, too. Kenny tries to sing like a burned-out rock star, but he has range, as Ms. Torres likes to say.

Arturo's music begins, and everyone shuts up and waits for the show. He never disappoints us. I recognize the tune after just three notes. It's "Bésame Mucho," the mushiest love song in the Spanish language. Even my mother, who had to sing it at every Latino event (since it's always in the ten-most-requested-songs category for Puerto Ricans, Cubans, Mexicans, Dominicans, Colombians, etc.), called it the

Suck-My-Face song. But why has Arturo picked this of all songs to sing? His reason soon becomes clear.

"This is my favorite love song," Arturo says into the microphone, which isn't even on. He is now using what he calls his Las Vegas performer voice and mannerisms, grasping the mike stand with both hands, lowering his eyes as if he were about to kiss someone. We all laugh. Even looking like a crash victim, he's a riot.

The lyrics to "Bésame Mucho" can make you gag like trying to swallow a lump of sugar, especially in translation. In Spanish they are merely nauseatingly sentimental; in English, they make you want to excuse yourself in a hurry. The rough translation of this song goes something like this: Kiss me, kiss me a lot. Kiss me as if this were the last time. Kiss me (high, high note), kiss me a lot, because I fear losing you. Kiss me . . .

Arturo begins to sing in a soft voice. He's looking down, and then he lifts his eyes like Madama Butterfly's fan and sweeps his gaze over to Kenny. My heart jumps. Arturo is going to get killed. And this time, I won't be there to save him. He sings for a full three minutes, looking at Kenny the whole time. Yolanda is staring at Kenny, too, an evil smile on her face.

Kenny stares straight ahead the whole time. He's like a statue. But the veins on his forehead have popped out.

Arturo sings the stupid song with so much passion that Ms. T. is wiping tears from her eyes by the time he finishes. To her it's not the words in a song but the feeling you put into it that matters.

At first there's total silence when Arturo finishes. Then Yolanda starts clapping like a maniac. The others join in. I watch Kenny turning red. When Arturo sits down next to me, I pinch his arm hard. I am furious with him. He just turns to me and smiles, but he is sad, I can tell. He's no fool. It's just that Arturo has to fight his battles his own way. I let my hand rest on his arm where I had pinched it. I love this boy, even though he is a puzzle I have to keep solving every day.

Ms. T. finally comes out of her trance. "Tomorrow we will have Doris and Yolanda sing," she says. "Kenny has signed up for Wednesday and the others have passed on the chance. *Bien*. Don't forget your taped music, girls. *Hasta luego.*"

Kenny stares at Arturo with so much disgust on his face that it frightens me. They lock eyes for a minute. It's as if they're communicating telepathically. And it's not good thoughts they're exchanging.

Kenny has made Arturo his target for years. We all grew up together in the barrio, but by the time we started high school some of us had become strangers to one another. Kenny has always been a bully, getting into trouble—his main means of self-expression. Bigger and stronger than the other kids, he didn't care what anyone thought of him, and has humiliated Arturo in a thousand different ways.

But this year it's different. Before, it had been a matter of taunts, name-calling, leading his pack of Tiburones gang members in some obscene cheer when Arturo walked by.

What happened in chorus is a good example of Arturo's method. He's always known that Kenny Matoa is a jerk. But lately, I had caught Kenny looking at Arturo with real hatred in his eyes, as if Arturo's existence was personally offensive to him. With the mugging, some kind of line has been crossed.

Arturo and I are walking to our lockers when Yolanda comes up.

"Cool song, Arturo," she says. "You made it sound new, you know."

"Hi, Yoli." Arturo seems distracted, looking up and down the hall teeming with a herd of loud kids rushing to their lockers. "Yoli, I never thanked you for your help the other night."

"No problem, *amigo*. You and I still gotta talk, right? Hey, Doris, you not speaking to me again? Didja get in trouble with your pops? I had to get rid of the evidence, you know, the bloody clothes, before my mom saw them and called the cops. On me, that is. She'd call them and ask if any of my friends had died a violent death recently. It's great when your mom has so much faith in you, ain't it? Uh, sorry, Doris, I forgot your mother . . . went on an extended vacation."

"Bye, Yolanda." I am having one of my old spooky feelings as I listen to her go on, talking fast, acting like a punk, putting on a show for anybody walking by. Maybe my mother had been right about Yolanda. Doña Iris, too. This girl is *loca* and dangerous. "You coming, Arturo?"

"Guys, wait." Yolanda blocks our way. "I miss hanging out with you. Both of you. Look, my mom's out, why don't you come over to my place? I've got something to tell you. Something important."

"I don't know, Yolanda. I'm in enough trouble already. My father wants to have a serious talk with me tonight. You know what *that* means. I've got to get home early."

"I'll go, Yoli," Arturo says. He sounds like a little boy. He is still shaken from his face-off with Kenny, I can tell. But Yolanda is not the stabilizing influence he needs. That would be me. So I'm trapped. I follow Yolanda home.

The wooden box is sitting on the coffee table again. Had Yolanda planned this scene ahead of time, laid it out for us?

Yolanda lights up a cigarette. Like a sleepwalker, Arturo opens a window. He always does that when someone smokes indoors. Then we sit down in a circle like ladies about to have tea or something.

"So what is it that you want to tell us?" I have to get this conversation going so I can go home to prepare myself for my big number with Papi. I can sense that Yolanda is on edge by the way she is watching her cigarette burn out.

She announces dramatically, "It's my last one." Her smile seems out of place on her pale and tired-looking face. "I'm pregnant," she says.

"You're going to have a baby?" Arturo is actually grinning like an idiot, and staring at Yolanda's middle.

"That's what it usually means, Arty." Yolanda's big smile is a big put-on. I can tell without having to read her mind.

"But you told me that . . ." I am going to remind her about her miscarriage when I remember that it's a secret.

"I lied, Doris. I didn't have a miscarriage. I just wasn't ready to admit my *delicate condition* even to myself. I was hoping it'd go away. Now I know I want to keep it."

"Did you tell Kenny?"

"Yeah, I told him. And you know what he said? 'That's *your* problem, Yoli.' I told him *our* baby is not a problem. It's gonna be a better human being than his father!"

"Does your mother know?" I suddenly understand the baggy clothes.

"Not yet. She hasn't been home much. She's in love with a *jíbaro*-hick just up from the island and they go out a lot. I'm waiting for school to end. I'm not going back next year, but it's too much hassle to quit now. Besides, there's a little matter I want to take care of. I thought you guys might be interested in helping me."

An alarm goes off inside my head: *Danger, land mines ahead.*

"I have my own problems, Yolanda. I guess if you're happy about the baby . . ."

She doesn't let me finish.

"Doris, don't be such an idiot. You think that because your moms took off with that *sinvergüenza* Geraldo and your pops is going out with the fat singer, you have the exclusive rights to the title of Messed-up Kid with the Most Problems? You don't *know* problems, girl. Try mine for a day. See how it feels. I'm not asking you for nothing anymore. Why don't you go home to Papi? You're a good girl. Mami is the bad girl in your family. Am I right?"

I jump at her, but she has already reached for the box on the table between us.

"Go home, Doris. I have something to show Arturo."

That's fine with me. I have things to do, too, like going home and taking a long bath and trying to think of other things besides Yolanda and her crazy life.

Doña Iris is already in her lawn chair when I go up to the roof. She looks like a mummy wrapped up in a thick shawl, even though it's warm, muggy even.

"She won't let me touch her, Doris."

"What?" She must have expected me to have read her mind. I had been thinking of letting her take care of the pigeons by herself, permanently, even though she's not looking too sturdy these days. It's a job I don't want to inherit.

"Martha is hurt. Her foot is bleeding and one wing is broken. She won't let me get close."

All of a sudden, I am afraid that if Martha dies, it'll kill Doña Iris. All she has now are these birds, and Martha is their leader and queen. I surprise myself by how nervous I am, scared to look and discover bad news. I walk carefully toward the bird condo. Martha is hiding in her coop. I have to reach in and cup her completely with both hands. She makes strange hissing sounds, and her pulse seems too fast, even for a bird. She tries to wriggle out of my hands. I stroke her feathers while I examine her closely. One wing's drooping, and her right foot does have dried blood on it.

Doña Iris brings me a pan filled with water from the cooler we keep for bird supplies. I place Martha gently in the pan and pour handfuls of water over her.

"What happened to her?"

"*No sé.* How can one know? There are many dangers in the world, and even if you have wings you can't always escape them."

I put Martha gently back in her coop. She is calmer, but her head drops into her chest feathers.

"What can we do for her?" I ask, rubbing Martha's little head gently with my fingertips.

"Nothing more than what we are doing. Make her comfortable. Feed her. Let her heal, if she's going to heal. Let her die, if she has to die. Everybody's time comes sooner or later, whether they are ready or not. Last night I dreamed of teeth. In my dream I saw the ground strewn with teeth. They looked like small gravestones. To dream of teeth is a bad omen . . ."

It's all too depressing. To try to cheer her up, I read her a list of Puerto Rican song titles I found in the school's library. I listened to as many of these extreme love songs as I could stand—actually they are pretty good, although the themes get repetitive: broken heart, tears, wine, blood, betrayal, and more *amor, amor, amor, corazón, lágrimas, vino, sangre, traición, y más amor, amor, amor.* But it's their titles I really like. They read like a poem.

"Doña Iris. Listen to these. I can make up a whole story just from this list: 'Atrapado,' 'Brujería,' 'Bésame Mucho,' 'Celoso,' 'Cenizas,' 'Un Cigarillo, La Lluvia y Tú,' 'Cuando las Mujeres Quieren a los Hombres,' 'Cuando Vuelva a Tu Lado,' 'Devoradora de Hombres,' 'Hablando Sola,' 'Ingrato,' 'Ladrona de Amor,' 'Más Feo Que Yo,' 'No Llores, No Vuelvo,' 'Se Fue,' 'Somos Diferentes,' 'Soñando con Puerto Rico,' 'Mi Música Ehh.'"

In a sort of trance, Doña Iris starts chanting, "*Se fue, se fue, se fue.*" She is stuck on "He went away."

I try to distract her with an extemporaneous rendering of a story made from song titles. She likes *cuentos*, tall tales, of any kind. I'm hoping I can get her out of her altered state with performance poetry.

I stand in front of her and bow. I begin to recite in a deep, dramatic voice, marking my lines by flapping my arms like a band conductor to:

"The Witch's Spell," a poem by Doris

I am trapped in a witch's spell. *¡Bruja!*
Quick! Come *bésame mucho* and break it.
Hear my song. *La canción en español*
is always about love and always *triste*.
In it *llueven lágrimas*. Rain of tears.
No llores, corazón. Don't cry, my love.
Canta y no llores. I am your *cielito lindo*.
I dream of flying over *tu isla*. Feel a breeze?

Son mis alas, my wings.
You have your *canción*, and the sun,
and I have wings to fly.

"What do you think? Pretty bad, I know. Doña Iris?"
She has dozed off during my recitation. I leave her alone to rest while I sit and watch the evening fall and the pigeons come home. Then, suddenly, she gets up, looking flustered, as if she had forgotten to do something, or I had distracted her from an important task.

I leave Doña Iris fussing over Martha and muttering her nonsense about death. I don't know how much of her dooms-day attitude, talk of death, trances, and lectures about my so-called gifts I can take. I am fighting it, but a strange pressure is building inside my chest. I am beginning to understand my mother's rising sense of panic that this barrio would eventually suffocate her. If only *I* had wings.

My father and Ms. M. are sitting at the kitchen table, staring at the door, waiting for my entrance. I am sure he is going to grill me about the Saturday night incident, or the letter from school about my absences and "unusual appearance" (which had finally reached him after I had rerouted the first two envelopes to my room). It seems that Mrs. Latham had finally sent one to the Caribbean Moon. I have prepared my speech, mostly complaints about being left alone, guilt-inducing evidence about his neglect, a subtle hint or two that I could still request Family Services to investigate our home life—an empty threat, of course, but one that still might distract my father from my problems at school. But my father appears more distraught and afraid than angry. Margarita is holding both his hands on the table. They look like they have been channeling really disturbed spirits from the Great Beyond.

"Doris, where have you been?" he asks me in a choked-up voice. It really scares me. I immediately think bad news, a *tragedia*. My mother? Heart attack? I sit down quickly because my knees are about to buckle. My stomach cramps up.

"*¿Qué pasa?*" My emergency Spanish comes out of my mouth automatically. I sound just like Mami, even to myself. "Is something wrong?"

They look at each other. I really hate it when adults collude (a word I got from a TV crime show, meaning "to plot") right in front of you. They're communicating about me without speaking. I'm about to vomit from anxiety.

"Where have you been today, Doris?" It's Margarita asking the question, her deep voice calm, her eyes trying to reel mine in.

"School, where else?"

"After school, until now. Where did you go?"

"I was with Arturo and Yoli. Then I went up to the roof. What's this all about? Is something wrong? Is it about Mami?"

Papi looks sort of stunned and scared at the same time. It's Margarita who finally responds to my questions with questions of her own.

"Can you tell us exactly where you were with your friends? Doris, what's the story here?" Margarita delivers these questions as if she has rehearsed them. They may have originally been my father's script, but he seems incapacitated.

I've had enough of the melodrama, and I get up, pushing my chair away so hard it falls over. "I am not answering any more questions until I get some answers myself. What is going on?" I am screaming by this time.

Margarita rushes over to me and places her hands on my shoulders. I realize that I'm trembling. I have the urge to let her hold me until my chest quits hurting. But I snap back to reality just in time, and push her away.

"Don't touch me!"

She doesn't give up. Instead she takes both my hands and pulls me down to sit at the table where my father remains frozen, staring at both of us. Margarita picks up the overturned chair, and taking a long, deep breath, she says: "Doris, there has been a shooting. The police found the gun. They know it was registered to Yolanda's late father, and witnesses saw you with Arturo and Yoli after school."

I can't believe what she's saying. My father has put his hands over his face and seems to be crying.

"Who got shot?" I shout, and then when he doesn't answer, I say, "Papi! You don't think I go around shooting people, do you? Has everybody gone crazy? If Mami were here, she'd be laughing at both of you for thinking such a thing about me. Who got shot?" I've jumped up from the table by then, but Margarita pulls me back down again. I push her hands off me. I feel trapped in a nightmare.

"Stay still and listen, Doris." She doesn't touch me again, but her voice has a deadly serious tone, so my body goes into automatic pilot and I sit back in my chair. My father clears his throat and begins to speak in a shaky voice: "*Hija*, the police officers came by about twenty minutes ago and said they needed you to go to the police headquarters for questioning and fingerprinting. They are testing the gun for fingerprints and trying to find a match with *evidence* they expect to find on the weapon."

The way he says *evidence* terrifies me. I imagine myself in an orange jumpsuit, handcuffed and shackled, being dragged away to prison for a crime I did not commit! "Papi, please. *Por favor*, don't act like I'm guilty! You know I don't even like guns! They scare me!" But then I remember I held the gun the other night. I feel like I am having a hallucination. You always hear people say in the 911 emergency shows that when they find themselves in a terrible situation, they feel like they are hovering above their own bodies, watching the awful thing happen around them.

"They said that Kenny Matoa was shot during an act of vandalism."

"Kenny, shot? What do you mean, an act of vandalism?"

"It was at El Bazar, the clothing store. He was throwing a brick or rock or something through the glass when somebody shot him from behind."

"*¡Dios mio!* Is he dead?"

"No. He's hurt pretty bad, though. Whoever did it didn't have good aim. They got him in the back and the bullet went right through him. The cops found the gun right there on the street."

A chilling calm is spreading over me. I come out of my fog like someone walking out of darkness into blinding light. El Bazar is the store where Arturo works part-time. My heart sinks at the thought that Matoa had finally pushed gentle, sweet Arturo to violence.

"So I'm one of the suspects." I slip easily into my TV cop show mode. People who think TV doesn't teach you anything are wrong. We all have parts to play, and these shows give us the role-playing vocabulary. I amaze myself at how much I already know about this episode I am now living through—the only piece that's a little foggy is the ending.

"*Sí*. And the other two suspects are your friends, Arturo and Yolanda." My father reaches for my sweaty hand. I let him hold it like a limp dead fish. I know Arturo well enough to know that his walking around the city alone at night, and what he had done to humiliate Kenny, were his ways of surviving the relentless abuse, of proving that he is not a coward. Had he finally had enough of Kenny's bullying? Was he capable of shooting someone in the back? Or had Yolanda done it because of the baby?

I can't help myself and start crying.

My father jumps up. "Doris, did you have anything to do with this? *Por Dios, hija*. I know I've left you alone a lot, and your mother . . . never mind her. It's my fault for not being here for you. *¿Verdad?* Isn't this right? But what did he do to you, this Matoa hoodlum? Did he . . . Doris, say something!"

Margarita makes him sit down again. She has been hovering between us like a referee.

"Papi, how can you believe I shot anybody? I did hold the gun the other night, but I told you I left Arturo and Yoli and went up to the roof this afternoon." By now I'm bawling like a baby. I want, I need, my mother. She loves high drama. She would know how to handle this without going to pieces.

"You held the gun! How . . ."

"Let her speak, *mi amor.*" Margarita nods in my direction, commanding me with her eyes, *Get control of yourself.*

I shoot her a dirty look for daring to call my father *her* love in front of me. I am in control. Anger does that to me; it focuses me. I walk out of the room with my head up, just like Mami would have done.

Doña Iris vouched that I was with her at the time of the shooting, so the police don't bother to get my fingerprints. Apparently she managed to be coherent. But Arturo is being held in custody. Kenny insists he had seen him running away from the scene. "I know him. He runs like a girl," he told the police officer who had questioned him. The officer—Perez—happens to be a friend of Papi's. He has Papi bring me to his office. He had heard ¡Caliente! play at a buddy's wedding. He and my father got tight quick. Papi has been getting the fast-breaking bulletins directly from him.

Checkout receipt.
Mead Public Library-Circ B
710 North 8th Street
Sheboygan, WI 53081

Customer ID: ****221626

Title: If I could fly
ID: 9001043266
Due: Saturday, October 15, 2011

Total items: 1
9/17/2011 12:26 PM

For renewals, call 920-459-3400, ext.
3401. You will need your library card. Or,
visit us at www.easicat.net, log in to your
account, and renew at the Items Out
window.

Late fees will be charged as follows:
$0.20 a day/$9.00 maximum PER
ITEM=Adult & Young Adult Materials
$0.15 a day/$20.00 maximum per ITEM=
Rental DVDs & Books
$0.05 a day/$6.00 maximum per ITEM=
Children's Materials

So Arturo has been fingered by Kenny as the shooter. He had no alibi since he had "gone for a walk" alone after leaving Yolanda's place. He told the police that Yolanda had tried to get him to take the gun "to scare Kenny a little," but he had refused.

Yolanda isn't talking except to say that she doesn't know anything about anything. Her pregnancy is now public, since her mother had to rush her to the emergency room after she started complaining of severe cramps after the shooting happened. I heard that her mother had fainted when the doctors told her that her daughter was well on her way to making her an *abuela*.

Before leaving the precinct house, I'm allowed to see Arturo. Well, actually, I refuse to budge from my chair until Perez makes a call, and a hostile-looking woman in a blue police uniform takes me into a claustrophobic room in the back. All expense has been spared in the decor here. He's sitting at a tacky plastic green table. He looks green himself. To put Arturo in such an ugly space is cruel and unusual punishment. He is so sensitive about his environment. The policewoman points to a chair across from him. She stands behind him, pretending not to be listening. But her ears practically vibrate like antennae. Arturo looks more like a skinny little boy than ever. He's still wearing his black silk shirt and Versace jeans, but they seem odd in this room.

"Doris, *¿qué pasa?*" His smile is the most unconvincing one I have ever seen, like someone pretending to be cheerful through a bad toothache.

"Arturo . . ." I break down in tears. I can't help it. "Arturo, how much time did you get?"

"Doris, don't be silly. I haven't been charged, much less convicted. I'm just being held for questioning. My mother is talking to somebody right now. I'll be out by tonight."

"And then what?"

"I don't know, Doris. Lieutenant Perez says Kenny is trying to get his mother to press charges."

"Did you do it? Did you just snap under the pressure?" These, I know and he knows, are lines right off the little screen in my living room. But I have no better way of asking my questions. My life has turned into an episode of a reality crime show.

"I didn't do it, Doris."

"Then why are you in here?"

"Kenny and a couple of his Tiburones swore they saw me running off after the shooting."

"They lied, right?" Why do I bother to ask that stupid question? Does Kenny lie? That's like asking whether sharks are meat eaters.

Arturo shrugs. "I think Yolanda did it: she's in a bad way. Emotionally, I mean. When I left her, she kept talking about convincing Kenny to marry her. Can you believe it? She's fifteen and he's sixteen going on three—in mental age, that is."

"Arturo," I whisper, "you have to tell the cops. You can't take the rap for Yolanda."

"I'm not going to jail, Doris. I never touched the gun, so they won't find my prints on it."

"Did I tell you that I think you'd look like a freak in an orange Day-Glo jumpsuit?" I tell him. "Orange is not your color, *querido*."

"If I have to do time, and I won't, I will fast until they change the uniform color to one more suitable to my complexion, *querida*. Okay?"

I hug him tight before leaving, so that he knows I love him.

That night I dream that I look in the mirror and I see my mother's face, her eyes, her mouth, and her wild black hair. I turn around, but no one else is there. Just me. I can see her only when I look in the mirror. I try talking to her, but it's my lips that move when she answers. I sing a love song in Spanish, and it is her voice that comes from my throat. Then someone knocks at the door for real, and Mami's face blends back into mine.

"Doris, do you need anything?" It's Margarita. I say nothing. She has driven my mother out of my dream.

8

When I get up, the apartment is empty, but my father has left a note for me to call Mami before I go to school. He's doing a show with Margarita at the Caribbean Moon tonight and rehearsing all day. As usual, he's left me several phone numbers, but this time he's added a PS: *I love you, Dorita.* I guess the possibility of seeing his only child on death row has opened his eyes a little. Margarita has added a P.P.S.: *There is a bowl of the* asopao *I made for dinner in the refrigerator. Heat it for 2 minutes.* She cooks fine, but I can't eat her food, not just yet. Good thing there is also old, left-over takeout.

Mami answers on the second ring.

"Mami." That's all I manage to say before I break down. I need help. In the few months she's been gone, I've turned into a slobbering fool.

She keeps saying things like *"Hija, hija, cálmate."*

After I do calm down, I tell her what's been going on. She

says she knows. Papi called her right away. She wants me there on the island with her. She'll make reservations for me, New York to San Juan tickets for the day after school ends.

"You want me to move there?" I have that old brochure of the island on my night table. I can see us on that pastel beach. I remember the sun from the last time I went to see Abuela. I had been a little girl then, and I had not liked the heat or the mosquitoes. But it could be different now. The sun would recharge my batteries: that's what Mami always said she needed, to recharge her batteries in the island sun. She and I could sing together and become famous as a mother-daughter act. People would ask, "Who's the mother?" "The prettier one," someone would always answer. I wouldn't mind letting her be a star like she has always wanted. I'll even help her get there.

"Doris, let's start slow, okay? Why don't you come stay with us for a few weeks after school is out and we'll see how it goes."

"If you don't want me there, just say so. You don't have to feel sorry for me. I'm okay." I am suddenly furious at her luke-warm offer. I guess she and Papi had decided I needed a little vacation.

"*Hija,* it's not what you think. My heart is in worse shape than they thought. I didn't want to alarm you before getting more tests done."

Fear that my mother may die and I will never see her again grips me.

"Mami, please let me take care of you. Are there good doctors in that town? Is Abuela with you?"

"I'm getting the best care, Dorita. I have good doctors and Mamá is a good nurse. It'll be great to be with you. We have a lot to talk about. I want to give you a CD I made. It has 'Cielito Lindo' on it."

"What about Geraldo?"

"He travels a lot. He is a talent agent now, too. You know musicians, *hija*, always moving."

"I love you, Mami."

"Are you singing, Doris?"

"I'm still in chorus. We're singing at graduation."

"Good. Having visions or dreams?" She laughs. "Has Doña Iris read your palm lately?"

Her voice is getting weaker, and I can tell she's tired, talking only for my sake.

"She says I'm going to fly over water soon, going on a journey, Mami."

Mami laughs softly. "I guess I was wrong about her, Doris. I guess she's the real thing."

At school, Arturo is *el hot Latino del momento*. Both of us are constantly pumped for information about our "arrests." Even the teachers are curious, except Ms. Torres, who seems oblivious to anything but the graduation program, which is coming up at the end of this week.

So Arturo and I are sort of celebrities. Not that shootings are rare in this neighborhood, but we're the *good* kids, the salvageable ones, so it's different. News about Yolanda's pregnancy hardly makes a ripple in the halls. And as for Kenny, the Tiburones are taking turns protecting him while he's in the hospital. They're wearing black armbands on their denim jackets, except in school, where there's zero tolerance for any public displays of gangsta bonding. The rumor is that Kenny has a damaged kidney, might need to have it cut out. After he recovers, he's being sent to an alternative school for the brick-throwing incident. But there's the little matter of who shot him to settle first.

Kenny had seen someone dressed in black running down the street after he was shot. Whoever it was had shot from an alley. There are plenty of witnesses who saw the shooter's back. Everyone remembered Arturo's black silk shirt. But only I remembered that Yolanda was wearing all black that day, too.

That afternoon, I meet Doña Iris on the roof. I tell her about my mirror dream.

"Mirrors are doors into another part of one's soul." She talks while holding Martha in her shaky hands and spreading the bird's injured wing out gently. "In a dream you can look into the mirror and see what is coming. Or what you fear is coming."

Okay. I had asked for an explanation, and I am getting the typical Doña Iris mumbo jumbo. Never a straight answer. She had been wrong about my so-called gift. I guess my mind-reading had been like the dream mirror Doña Iris is still mumbling about: I saw what I wanted to see, or what I feared I would see. But I don't need supernatural powers to see that Doña Iris is getting old and feeble. She can barely handle Martha.

"Doña Iris, I don't know if you've heard that I'm going down to the island to see my mother."

She doesn't say anything. She hands me the nervous bird. Martha is healing fast, but her wing is never going to be perfect again. Most of the feathers have not started to grow back over the scar tissue. Her coat of white and gray feathers is dull, not shiny as usual from preening. Where has Martha been? Who or what has hurt her? I hold her close to my chest, and it is like I have my own heart in my hands.

"Will she fly again?"

"Yes, *creo que sí*. I think so. But who can know how she feels?" Doña Iris has wrapped herself up in a sweater, though it's almost summer already and the roof is heating up like a grill. "But I do not think she will fly as far or as long as she used to."

We put Martha back into the nest box we made for her, filling it with straw and cedar chips. She seems restless. All the other birds are out for the day. I cover the opening of her nest box with a black cloth so she'll think it's night and sleep.

Doña Iris herself has fallen asleep on the lawn chair. Her mouth is open and her wispy gray hair has fallen on her forehead. For a moment, I can see how she must have looked as a child. I sit on a bag of feed watching her until she's awakened by a plane passing overhead. I have been thinking that the roof will be the only place I'll miss.

"*¿Hija?*" She seems confused. It worries me to think about what will happen to the birds if Doña Iris can't take care of them. I will have to mention it to Papi. Maybe he'll remember the promises he made to Don Pichón. But I let that thought go. I had wanted a plan for my life. Now I have one. Time for me to fly.

9

Kenny had to have the damaged kidney removed. Arturo is no longer a suspect because Yolanda admitted to the crime when the police found her fingerprints on the gun. Lieutenant Perez let her go home while they sort out the charges and made her promise not to go anywhere. He is counseling her personally. I'm still mad at her for not telling the truth in the first place, but that man is a saint. St. Perez of the Silver Badge. As for Papi and Margarita, it's the usual— play at the club at night and sleep most of the day. It seems like a good time for me to leave town. No one will even notice.

At graduation, I end up singing "El Jibarito" as a solo. Every Latino and Latina in the crowd has their handkerchiefs out by the time I hit the last note. Ms. T. hugs me hard backstage. She puts a script in my hands and tells me that in the fall she's going to direct a new, *modern* version of *West Side Story*, and that we're going to help her write it as a class project.

"And, Doris, you will be a perfect María!" Ms. T. is

obviously getting passionate about her new project. By fall, she'll be in a frenzy.

"Sounds great, Ms. Torres. Let me think about it, okay? You know I have stage fright."

"No way, Doris, you soar on the wings of angels when you are onstage singing."

Hyperbole is what my English teacher calls this kind of exaggeration. What would Latinos do without hyperbole?

"I promise I'll consider your idea seriously, even *passionately*, Ms. T."

I don't tell her that I'm not planning to be back in September. I'm just glad my voice sounds good and strong today. I say a little prayer to myself, making a *promesa* that if Mami recovers, we're going to take the island by storm. Then I'll talk her into a mainland tour. We'll send the first invitations to Papi and Margarita.

I go sit next to my father and Margarita, who has conspicuously saved a seat for me by putting her huge red purse on it. I could have stayed backstage, but I want to have a good view of Arturo singing a jazzed-up version of "Guantanamera" that has everybody rocking out in their seats. The school chorus does their thing next: our principal's choice, and our unofficial alma mater. *Ugh.* There are groans from the kids in the crowd, after the third time we hear "We are the world/We are the children." Luis Cintrón pretends he's choking, and one of his Tiburones gives him the Heimlich maneuver. There's the usual hugfest after the diplomas, and then I let my father drive me home. He and Margarita go on and on about how much talent I have. I pretend I'm sleeping in the back seat.

Doña Iris peeks out of her apartment when she hears me coming up the stairs. She hands me a paper bag. Then she makes the sign of the cross over my head.

"*Dios te bendiga, hija.* May you be safe in your journey. Here are two books and a rosary. Please return them to me when you are back home."

"I'll mail them back to you, Nana." I haven't called her Nana since I was a child, and I surprise myself when my baby name for her comes out of my mouth. She takes my face in her soft, wrinkled hands and kisses my cheek. She smells like an old book herself, kind of like a library smells, musty but familiar and safe.

"Doris, *hija.* I will take care of the birds until you return. Do not worry."

"*Gracias*, Nana." I hug her gently. Her head just barely reaches my chin. Her skin is so thin that I can feel her bones underneath, her fragile bird bones.

She goes inside her little apartment. I catch a glimpse of the table covered with an embroidered white cloth. I used to hide under there when she read people's fortunes. I heard everybody's stories. I knew everybody had their own secret life.

The two books she gave me are *How to Read People's Faces* and *Los Sueños*, a book in Spanish about interpreting dreams. The rosary is beautiful, amber beads joined by silver links and a silver crucifix. I have seen it in Doña Iris's hands all my life. It's her habit to finger the beads and mumble prayers all day.

When I get home, I open the book written in English first.

"To tell if someone is lying to you, you must watch their hands. People will show their hands freely when they have nothing to hide. But they will hide them in their pockets or behind their backs when they are afraid to give themselves away. Look at their eye movements: Are they shifting their pupils back and forth? This is a sign of a guilty conscience." I read on. I have to laugh. So this was one of the secret weapons of the fortune-teller. Doña Iris used to irritate me by watching my every move like she would a fascinating movie. She watched me eat, play, sleep. Then she'd surprise me by telling me that she knew I was worried, or sick, or lonely. She was almost always right. And all this time I thought she was reading my mind.

I wonder whether Lieutenant Perez reads books like this one, too. Then I have an idea. Tomorrow I am going to go around and say *adiós* to a few people. My ex-boyfriend, Danny, is one of them. I haven't talked to Danny in months, not since he transferred to Eastside High, but I've heard that he isn't going out with anybody yet. I skip to the section "How to Read Your Lover Like a Book." It says that lovers "preen," to show each other and others that they are a couple. The woman might arrange her body or chair to block out other people. She will toss her hair back, lick her lips, and thrust her chest forward toward the male. The man will try to look deep into the woman's eyes, reach to touch hands repeatedly, or place a hand on one of her body parts to signify exclusive rights. I have seen my parents doing all this. Then not doing it. Now it's *preening* time for Papi and Ms. M.

10

Daniel Santos Montoya is working as a delivery boy at the florist shop in the mall. So I wake up Saturday morning and I put on my mother's purple capri pants and a Puerto Rican Day Parade sweatshirt, spray on some White Diamonds, and set out to read Danny like a book. I take the bus there. I peek through the shop's glass door. He is wiping down the counter, and does he ever look good in a UPS uniform without the UPS tag. He must have picked it up at the thrift store. UPS guys have a reputation for looking sexy in those brown shorts. I guess Danny has heard that, too. I don't get it. Old guys showing off hairy legs is not attractive to me, not even acceptable. But Danny may be a different case. It's worth checking out closer up.

"Doris, hey!" He jumps over the counter when the buzzer on the door announces my entrance, which I hope is dramatic. He pulls me to the back room where the fresh flowers are kept in buckets and refrigerators, sort of like a weird garden, or maybe a flower morgue. He kisses me until my knees buckle. After a while I remind him, "Danny, hey! We broke up, remember?"

"Ah, yeah. Sorry, Doris. I forgot." He laughs and kisses me some more. I decide not to insist any further on the technicality of our breakup. After all, I have come here for a reason. What is it? The thinking distracts me from enjoying the kiss. It's going on too long, but I can't unglue myself from this very focused kisser. Danny jumps back when I pull his ear. He looks offended, but I'm just trying to let him know there's someone tripping the buzzer. I happen to come out front first, so this harried-looking guy in work clothes orders a dozen roses from me.

"What color?" I ask him.

"I guess roses are red. Gimme a dozen red roses."

"Right." Roses are red, violets are blue, every fool knows that, and if I don't take my wife some flowers tonight, I am history.

Danny wraps some roses from the fridge in white tissue, tucks them into a long box, and hands it to the guy. The man, looking worried, carries the long box out like a fishing pole or a rifle over his shoulder.

"So, Doris, want a job? You're good at this and I'm about to quit."

"Why?"

"I'm on the team. Made the Eastside team for next year. Gotta practice this summer."

The team is, of course, varsity basketball. Danny had been trying to prove to the coach at Central that even though he's a short Latino, he's got star quality. And he is fast and strong. I've never seen anybody jump and fly as high as Danny, an eagle with his eye fixed on the hoop, and the way he moves through a jumble of bigger players like a cat weaving through a herd of giraffes is worth filming for a nature show. I'm glad Eastside is giving him a chance.

"So what's new with you? Got a new boyfriend yet?" The place is empty and he's already getting ideas.

"Yeah. Ten or twelve. I was just passing by." I had considered telling Danny that my mother is gone, and my life is falling apart; after all, we had been close once, and I need a little sympathy and affection. That's why I'm standing in front of my ex. But when I look into his beautiful brown eyes, all I see are tiny basketballs bouncing around. He isn't going to listen to my troubles. He just wants to have fun.

"Want me to come by your place, Dorita, *mi vida, mi amor*? We could go up to the roof." He sounds like he's spoken these lines many times before.

His hands are on my waist, and it feels good. He has strong hands, Danny does. But I can tell that he's just practicing his game with me, not really into it.

"I'm busy with my new boyfriend, Danny." I lie. "You can get in line if you want."

"Hey, come to the games next year. Maybe I'll give you an autograph."

No, I am not going to be here next year. I think it but don't say it. What Danny's body language is saying to me is, *I'm immature. I'm more interested in basketball than in you, Doris.*

Let's talk about me *and we'll have a good time.* I am glad to
know body language. In my mind, I say *adiós* to Danny, my
first *amor.* Why should I waste my time with a boy when I
have my whole future ahead of me? On the island I will meet
interesting guys. Real men. They will appreciate me for my
talent. Wasn't that the way Papi had discovered Mami?

I give Danny a long goodbye kiss, just to remind him
what he's missing out on, and get on the bus home. No more
farewells for me. Too messy. *Ay bendito.* Like Martha, I'll just
take off toward the *cielito lindo,* and let others wonder
whether I will come home to roost.

When I get to the apartment, I start reading aloud the *West
Side Story* script that Ms. Torres gave me at graduation, just
so I can tell her why I can't do it. I spread the script out on
the kitchen table. I flip through it as I cook my dinner. I see
Ms. Torres's ideas and notes and Arturo's scribbled changes
in the margins and over the actors' lines. I see they have col-
luded to win me over to their crazy project. It means a lot to
Ms. T. because she wants to show her fellow teachers and the
mainstream students, as she calls the non-Latinos, that we
have loads of talent. "Tony, I gotta get out of this barrio before I go outta my mind . . ." says María.

Margarita comes out of the bedroom just as I'm getting
into the part.

"You want me to make you something to eat?" she asks,
like she's my mother.

"I already ate." I answer her without looking up.

"What'd you eat?"

"Tortilla."

Couldn't she see the eggshells on the counter, the dirty fry pan in the sink? Comfort food. I had made an omelet like Papi used to when he wanted to make things right. Ms. M. doesn't say anything but frowns like she's really disappointed. Why do some people take food so seriously? If you say no, they act offended. Looking at her wiping the counter with a tragic look on her face, I catch myself feeling sad for Margarita. She's trying hard to be a part of Papi's life. I almost say, *Okay, feed me.* But then something stops me. It's my mother's voice in my head. Singing.

Margarita finishes wiping the counter, starts a pot of coffee, and sits across from me at the table. She picks up the script.

"Want me to read Tony's part?" The woman can't take a hint.

"Sure."

So I watch her put on a macho attitude, puff out her chest—which is a pretty impressive sight—and cross her legs like a man; she isn't too bad at getting into Tony's character.

I forget my troubles playing María. It's really amazing how acting can take over your head. I guess it's like singing, like how Mami transforms herself into a star when she is onstage. It seems that the brain has a way of changing reality; it's like switching channels on a TV. If you believe, really work hard at believing, that you are happy, or powerful, or brave, or sick and miserable, you can make yourself be any of those things. When I look into Tony's (Margarita's) eyes, I believe there is someone out there who would die for my love. I try it, too. I tell "Tony" that we will escape this barrio, the gang violence, and live together happily in the real America. By the time we finish the scene, Margarita has tears in her eyes. Suddenly I realize how silly we look: I'm standing on a chair and she's on her knees singing "I Just Met a Girl Named María." We both burst out laughing.

It's the first time I feel that I am sharing real time with her, not just wishing Mami were here instead.

But as soon as we put away the script, wash up for the night, and settle down to watch a nature show on television—Margarita falls asleep, her head falling onto my shoulder so I have to push her off gently—the space that cannot be filled opens up again between us. I don't want to be here in this apartment with the woman who has replaced my mother in my father's life. I want . . . I don't know what I want, except to not be here with them anymore. Maybe what I want is to be like Mami, to get away from this barrio and start a new life, then *a volar*! Tomorrow I will take flight. No wings necessary; that's why jet planes were invented. Correct me if I'm wrong.

Part Three

Both sexes nest-call, but most commonly the male does so more often and at a higher intensity than the female. This is simply because he usually takes the lead in seeking a nest-site or in returning to one already selected.

11

I had spent the four-hour flight sleeping, and dreaming that my birds were following the plane, Martha leading them like a top gun. I'd read that racing pigeons can fly a five-hundred-mile race, close to half the distance between New York and the island. When the flight attendant pushed the button to raise my seat to the upright position, I awoke facing the clouds. I thought I saw Martha and her troops nesting on them.

Abuela picks me up at the San Juan airport's baggage terminal. She is wearing an outfit obviously intended to stun the unsuspecting passersby: a parakeet-yellow dress with fuchsia high-heeled shoes and matching purse that are as subtle as a carnival tent. I feel my pupils contract as she rushes toward me. I'm in my favorite baggy shorts and Mami's off-the-shoulder black sequined blouse. Since I had read that you should wear comfortable, practical shoes while flying (in case of an air disaster—high heels would poke holes in the inflatable air slide), I am wearing my old black antique Converse high-top sneakers, a thrift store once-in-a-lifetime find.

The first thing out of my fashion-conscious *abuela*'s mouth is the standard Puerto Rican all-purpose lament: "*¡Ay bendito!*"

To her credit, she does hug me like she means it. But the last time she saw me, at the funeral of her second husband, Mami had dressed me up like a señorita so I'd make a good impression. I mean, I had worn ankle socks with my white sandals! Mami had explained that we did not want to upset Abuela by making a fashion error while she was grieving. She said that when it's somebody else's day, even if he's dead, you do what you have to do to keep the peace.

The main thing I remember about Abuela is that she had a prepackaged saying for everything. She quotes old proverbs like some people quote the Bible or stock market prices. My mother had quoted her favorite one to amuse me while we were putting together my funeral costume: *Cantar bien o cantar mal, en el campo, indiferente. Pero delante de la gente . . . cantar bien o no cantar.* You can sing well or badly alone in the countryside, but when you have an audience, you better sing well or not at all.

It's been three years since we flew down for the funeral. It had been a short weekend trip, and I remember nothing except the heat, the crowd at the cemetery, the crowd at Abuela's. And getting in trouble for helping myself to the rum and Cokes being passed around at the reception. I was ignorant of this interesting cultural custom, though. I did not know there was eighty proof in the cups, I just knew I was thirsty. I got so sick that I spent the last day there with my head in the toilet—the porcelain sea. That had been my final view of our *isla*, my mother's idea of paradise.

Right after her *"¡Ay bendito!"* and a not-too-subtle disapproving glance, Abuela tells me that we are going straight to a fiesta in our pueblo. Mami is singing with the combo from the university. We have two hours to get there if we leave immediately. She looks me over again.

"Maybe we can stop by the house quickly so you can change your clothes, *niña*." She says this in a sweet voice. "If I can find my house again, that is. This is my first time driving alone all the way to San Juan." She shrugs her shoulders and says, *"Preguntando se llega a Roma."* You can find Rome just by asking for directions.

After asking three people how to get out of the airport, we are finally on our way. San Juan is a maze, though, and it takes two more stops before we find the *autopista*, the main highway through the island. I try to help Abuela by reading the map, but she's not interested in line drawings, she tells me. At one of the million toll booths she gets into such a complicated discussion with the attendant that a line of cars forms behind us. She and the woman are talking about the disgraceful way that some people dress in the capital. The other woman is bulging out of her Department of Transportation uniform, but she points out to Abuela that it's perfectly ironed, the creases as sharp as Gillette single-edged blades. It's only when they are shouting over blaring car horns, and the man in the jeep behind our car yells obscenities out of his window, words I am trying to memorize for future reference, that I begin to get a little nervous. When he starts to get out of his car, I finally tap my *abuela* on her arm and point to the chaos she's causing.

"*Ay, niña, con paciencia se gana el cielo.* Yes, yes. Even a sinner will get into heaven if she's patient enough," she says, giving the man pounding on the trunk of her car a look of total disdain. If you win heaven by being patient, that guy is going in the opposite direction.

She leisurely takes the coins from her purse and hands two quarters to the attendant, who is now glancing worriedly at all the rude drivers in her lane. Tough job. Collecting dirty money and dirty looks all day.

I decide right then and there that I will have to remember that patience proverb in order to survive in my grandmother's house.

Of course it takes almost three hours, not two, to get to her pueblo, which is only about fifty miles away. The town is packed with cars. Abuela basically intimidates other drivers out of her path all the way to the plaza. Her orange Toyota has no dents. Proof, she tells me, that she is not a bad driver. We don't have time to go by the house so I can change, and she doesn't mention it again, so I don't volunteer. People are just going to have to get used to my personal style around here. During the ride she has grilled me about myself, and especially the *problema* with the gun. And last but not least, my father's new girlfriend.

"Margarita is not a bad person." I surprise myself by saying this. But then I notice her look of contempt. Abuela seems quick to pass judgment on my father, or maybe she's just possessive. After all, Papi has been part of her family, too.

"What about Geraldo?" I ask. It isn't as if Mami had left us to join a convent.

"He and your *mami, son como el aceite y vinagre.* They are oil and vinegar, they want to be together, but they don't mix. He will be here tonight. You will see what I mean. *Ay bendito.* He is after gold on this island, just like the conquistadores. She wants to sing. He thinks that she will lead him to gold."

Abuela keeps on saying things I don't quite get. And not because she's speaking mostly in Spanish. When she sees I am totally confused, she switches to her basic English. Mami has explained that Abuela's generation grew up under the U.S. law that only English be spoken in school on the island. So now when the older people speak in English, they sound like they have swallowed a dictionary.

"Geraldo, he is an *oportunista,*" Abuela says as we park her orange Toyota under a NO SE ESTACIONE sign. Even though it says "No Parking," it's the only free spot in the center of town, she explains. When we come to the edge of the crowd gathered around the raised stage, I hear my mother's voice before I see her. She's saying that she and the musicians have decided to give the pueblo a special musical gift that night. They'll be playing only old Puerto Rican songs, the ancient tunes first recorded on pancake-thick vinyl albums. She will begin with one dedicated to her daughter, freshly arrived on the island.

"Doris, if you are out there, this is for you, *mi amor*!"

There's a scattering of applause. Abuela and I can make our way toward the front of the plaza because a bunch of people, mostly teenagers in punk clothes, are noisily moving away from the stage. I hear one say, "What's this crap? I thought they were going to have real music tonight."

The poster for the concert has a huge picture of a rap group called Los Bien Muertos. I think it means "the good and dead." The poster has a tiny picture of Mami and the combo under the name of the rap group. So I guess my mother is the opening act for them.

She sings her own interpretation of an old song called "Palomita Blanca." It's about a white dove that brings Jesus a gift of oil and vinegar in his beak. The refrain is about how in return, Jesus will tell him *la verdad*, the truth and only the truth. Not that I really understand all the lyrics, but I know what *la verdad* means.

I am always looking for *la verdad*, too. But how much will it cost me? Is the gift I bring my mother—of me, and my little bit of talent—going to be accepted or rejected? I smile at my own foolish need to fly here in case this is where the answers are. Am I a silly bird, a *palomita* bearing something bright in my beak, looking to buy myself a little truth? My *abuela* smiles, too. First at me, then at her daughter singing her failing heart out on the stage. She is proud. I want my mother to look like this at me.

The set is short. I meet Mami behind the stage. When I see her up close, I am shocked at how thin she is. Her gorgeous red dress is hanging on her.

She hugs me for a long time.

"That's beautiful music, Mami."

"Thank you, Doris. I sang 'Palomita Blanca' for you, but it was your *abuela* who requested it. That song is as old as . . . well, old. Not really in my public repertoire."

I look over at my devious *abuela*. She'd been talking about vinegar and oil earlier. I'd been too distracted to notice that she had been making a point in her own weird way about Geraldo. I should have known from reading Doña Iris's book on how to read people by what they say in between their words that Abuela was telling me that there is tension between my mother and Geraldo.

I spot him heading for us. He looks hot and annoyed. The gel in his hair is melting and he's wiping it off his forehead with a big handkerchief. He still looks like a greasy street thug in his low-cut Italian loafers, see-through socks, shiny black pants, and black silk shirt. My mother turns toward him, but does not really look at him. He comes closer. He smells of musk cologne and sweat. He gives me a big fake wolf smile.

"Doris, you're so grown up," Geraldo says. "It's only been a few months, but I hardly recognized you. I recognized your mother's blouse, though." He looks at my chest when he says that. I hear my grandmother mumble something to my mother, probably a proverb about men and boobs.

"Hi," I say without enthusiasm, careful not to make eye contact. I imagine him as a flea-bitten dog with rabies. No way I can ignore him, but I don't have to get near him, either.

"Tell me, Doris, did you enjoy the old song your mother sang tonight?" The sarcastic way that he says "old song" makes me cringe. My mother comes over to stand next to me.

"Yes, I did. Why?"

"Geraldo thinks that I'm wasting my time with these cultural revival programs, Doris. He thinks I ought to sing new music. It's what people pay to hear."

"This event tonight is a freebie for your mother and her combo, Doris. The next act is getting paid very well. Tell me, Doris, do you still sing? There's a market for young singers on this island."

"A gold mine yet to be explored. *Mina de oro. Mal de ojo*," Abuela says in a sarcastic tone that matches Geraldo's, as she crosses herself against the evil eye that can be summoned by greed.

I have to laugh, in spite of myself. Abuela's words are a samurai sword she points in Geraldo's direction.

Geraldo gives her a dirty look, which only encourages Abuela to strike again. She makes the sign of the cross in the air. Devil, be gone! This is a reckless man as well as an ignorant one. Beware, Geraldo, bearer of the evil eye, I say to myself, for you will be vanquished by La Abuela the Brave's arsenal of protective charms and spells.

"Señora, I am making your granddaughter an honest offer. Since your daughter is not really interested in a career in music."

My mother sighs as if she were exhausted. She is pale and tired-looking.

"Geraldo, this is not the time or place for this conversation. Why don't you come over to the house tomorrow, and we can talk. Doris and I have a lot of catching up to do before we make any decisions."

"I will come over if it's acceptable to your dear mother."

"*Al ladrón darle las llaves.* May as well hand over your house keys to the determined thief." Abuela shrugs her shoulders and takes my arm. Mami leads us away from the thundering herd of rappers and the rock band heading toward the stage.

"Yes, yes, *hija*," Abuela says, looking back at Geraldo. "Why not just give the thief your house keys? Why not?"

Mami looks at me as if to say, *That's your* abuela, *you know how she is.* But I can tell all is not perfect in her island paradise.

The town is teeming with people. There will be music for everyone, the posters announce. Rap, the old tunes, salsa from Nueva York, and island hip-hop. After some death-defying maneuvers on the winding road that leads to her house, moves that have *me* crossing myself and whispering a few prayers of my own, Abuela pulls into her driveway. She goes around to help Mami out of the car. I am getting worried about how pale and weak she looks.

Inside the house, after all the windows have been opened and the ceiling fans turned on so that curtains are flapping like wings, my mother calls me into her air-conditioned bedroom. I am glad she has this little luxury. I stand in front of the window unit, letting the cool air dry my arms. I will miss many things about my American life, AC on demand being near the top of the list.

"Doris, we have a lot to talk about, but I am tired from the show. We will talk tomorrow, okay? I am so happy you are here, *mi amor*." She hugs me for a long time. I smell her usual smell of White Diamonds, but the electricity that I used to feel vibrating inside her body is not there.

"I will be here a long time, Mami. I have a lot to tell you, too."

I help her climb up on the tall poster bed. She lets me tuck her in, the sly smile I know so well on her lips.

"Doris, isn't it funny how it is with mothers and daughters? I came home and my mother takes care of me like I took care of you when you were little. And now you are taking care of me? It's a matter of taking turns, you know?"

I nod, but I don't really agree with her. Did she ever take care of me? She didn't neglect me, but I am still waiting for her to ask me what *I* need.

Abuela is sitting in the living room. A small table fan is going full blast, aimed right at her face, so that she looks like she's a gray bird flying against the wind, her thick hair blowing back.

"Dios mío," she says. "This sun is a penance for all of us sinners. But I tell you something. I'd rather die by fire than by ice. I'd rather melt here than face one of your winters. Come here, Doris." She points to the chair next to her, also facing the fan. The fan is aimed at my face, and when I sit down, the gale wind from the fan slaps me back.

"I put fans in your room too, *hija*. You will sleep in a cool heaven tonight."

"Abuela, is Mami really sick?"

"*Sí, niña.* A heart condition, which she got from her father, my first husband, *que descanse en paz*, may he rest in peace. The doctor says she can live for many years, but he cannot say how many. It depends on how well she takes care of herself." My grandmother's voice changes as she says this. She looks away from me and brings her hand to her throat. The book Doña Iris gave me says that this gesture means that a person is trying not to cry, keeping the grief inside. I am beginning to wish I had not read this book. It's as bad as having the dreams I used to have when I believed I had a gift.

"So is she supposed to stay in bed? Why is she working if she's so sick?"

"Singing is what she loves to do, Doris. You know this. If she stops singing, she will die sooner. I believe this. I have always known that Claribel's talent is also a curse. *Pero, no hay rosas sin espinas.*" If you want a beautiful rose, you have to accept the thorns, too. I see her hand go to her heart. I don't have to look up that gesture in my book to know what it means.

"Doris, if you are here to take your mother back north to the barrio, I will have to tell you plainly that it will kill her."

"Abuela, I am here to stay with her. I need her. We can sing together . . ."

For some reason I burst out crying then. I should have put my hand to my throat, too, and kept the flood back.

139

Abuela moves closer and puts her arms around me and lets me cry on her chest. Then she pulls a hanky out of her robe's pocket and wipes my face as if I were a baby.

"I cannot tell you what to do. You are a señorita now. At fifteen years old I was already engaged to be married. It was a mistake, but I was sure I knew what was good for me then. Like you are now. Your mother has a dream. The hunger for fame is now a need to sing and to live. I will take care of her so she can live for her music, for as long as God lets her stay . . ." I hear her voice breaking, then she turns away, heading toward the kitchen. I watch her pour herself a shot from her adults-only cough medicine. She drinks it in one gulp.

She winks at me. "Doris, tomorrow *el caballero* Geraldo is coming to drive us to San Juan. There is a concert in the park."

"Will she be able to get through it?"

"If she sleeps well tonight, perhaps she will have the energy. Geraldo thinks that it's important for her to sing in the capital. I think he just wants to scout for other acts. I have told Claribel that the man is only interested in money. But she thinks that she owes him something. I decided to let him hang himself. I will not say anything else. Like I always say, *No eches más leña al fuego.*"

Right, I think. Abuela telling herself not to add wood to the fire is like waiting for a snowfall on this island, a snowball's chance in . . . I cut off the thought because I am in real danger of becoming a cliché-machine like my *abuela*. It's contagious.

* * *

That night I dream that Martha has flown across the Atlantic to visit me. She has a piece of paper in her beak. It is a picture of a rose on a long stem with thorns. The rose in the picture turns into a real flower that I pick up. As soon as I take it in my hand, it begins to shrivel up and turn brittle. I am left holding just a few painful thorns. Frightened by my cries, Martha flies out the window, flapping her wings violently and cooing in distress.

12

I finally pull myself out of the nightmare, only to find that the sheer white curtains in my room have gotten tangled up in the blades of the overhead fan. I turn the fan off and climb on the bed to undo the knotted curtains. Back in bed, I listen to the sounds of morning breaking, so different here than in our apartment building back in the city. Right before the sun comes up, I hear the song of the *coquí*, the thumb-size frog that sounds like it swallowed a foghorn: *co-quí, co-quí, co-quí*. A rooster crows, then another; the neighbors turn on a radio and sing along with it. A vehicle with huge loudspeakers announcing fresh bread for sale goes around and around. Then I hear my mother's voice singing and I smell the coffee brewing. I stay in bed, listening to my mother talk with her mother about me. How tall she's gotten, my *abuela* says. I smile. I am five-two, only tall when I stand next to my super-short mother and grandmother. Mami tells Abuela that I sing like an angel, too. She wonders whether I will sing a duet with her today in San Juan. She begins to sing "El Jibarito." That was the song I had performed at graduation, she tells Abuela.

I come out and join her in the chorus. We're both in our pajamas. Abuela does a Spanish waltz for us in her pink nightgown. By the time we finish the song, we're all laughing like crazy women.

We have not heard Geraldo come to the door. He's clapping. "The wolf always comes early to the sheep's dance," says Abuela, disappearing into her bedroom.

"Doris, not bad, you're sounding good, ladies. Yes, yes, I think it would be a good idea to have you sing at the concert today. With a little practice, you can turn professional in no time."

Abuela comes back with our robes, giving Geraldo a killer *mal de ojo*—the old evil eye—for having barged in on us without announcing himself while we are still in our nightclothes.

Mami is sitting down at the table, breathing kind of hard. I pour her a cup of coffee. Geraldo sits down to wait for his cup. Abuela looks like she wants to pour the whole steaming pot over his head. But she puts a cup down on the table, making him come get it himself. He is still staring at me. It's like he's just discovered I exist.

"Gonna introduce you to the Puerto Rican hip-hop scene, Doris. You won't believe it, girl. It's almost as big as in the city. Your mother hates it, you know. She thinks salsa is the only thing going."

"It's just what I'm good at, Geraldo." My mother seems to

be perking up, maybe with the caffeine in her system. "Doris is going to sing one song with me today. She can't do any more without rehearsing. Anyway, I have a program worked out with the combo."

"The combo, the stupid combo!" Geraldo scrunches his face in anger and shouts. "It's a bunch of college kids who play as a hobby. They're not pros. They're gonna be lawyers and dentists when they finish school. Then what? I thought you had ambition, Claribel!"

Abuela has come to stand next to my mother with her arms crossed over her chest. I know what it means: "I'm ready for a fight." My mother winks at me to let me know she is in control.

"Geraldo, we will be ready to leave in one hour. Please go somewhere and give this some thought: my contract with you says I will pay you 30 percent of everything I earn for my performances. I have been living up to that, have I not?"

Geraldo looks at her as if he wants to curse her out, but then he sees that my grandmother is cutting a loaf of bread into small slices with a very big knife. She is making as much noise as possible doing this.

"Breakfast is the most important meal of the day, *se lo aseguro*. Yes, yes. I know this for certain," she announces.

"See you in one hour, Geraldo," Mami calls out just before we hear his car screeching down the road.

His name is not mentioned while we eat the most important meal of the day. We discuss what to wear. In this country, my *abuela* explains to me, you are judged by your clothes.

"I don't think it's just in *this* country, Mamá," says my mother. I see that she is trying hard to act like nothing is wrong. But her hands tremble so much that she spills her coffee, and when her mouth smiles, her eyes remain sad.

"Doris, look in my closet and choose something you like. Just remember that it will be an outdoor show. It'll be hot, okay?"

Geraldo drives like a maniac, crouching over the wheel and taking every opportunity to upset Abuela. She and I are in the back seat. She keeps her eyes on his head as if she were drilling into his skull. Occasionally, an *"¡Ay, Dios mío!"* escapes her clenched lips. Mami has a CD playing, and she is practicing the songs she will sing that day. They are going to do a romantic ballad program to honor the legendary Puerto Rican singer Daniel Santos. The list of titles she shows me makes my heart leap up! I recognize some of them from the list I made for Doña Iris: "Historia de un Amor," "Mucho Corazón," "Vuélveme a Querer," "Amor Ciego," "Quiéreme Mucho," "Amor, Amor, Amor." Mami sings them with her eyes closed, her voice sweet and high. I pick up on the refrains. Geraldo looks like he's in pain the whole time we are singing. Once, when we stop to use the bathroom at El Burger King, he puts in a nueva salsa CD. It's a repetitive track, heavily mixed with electronic burps and gulps, and punctuated by what sounds like a frog in the singer's throat, like maybe she swallowed a *coquí: uh-huh, uh-huh, uh-huh, salsa para mí, salsa para ti, uh, uh, uh.*

"This singer's on the show today," Geraldo says, glancing back at me while passing a car in a double-yellow-line zone.

"*Ay, ay, ay,*" says Abuela, shaking her head in mock despair and squeezing my hand.

"Who is on the show?" Mami asks.

He doesn't answer her, but hands back the CD cover. The artist is a fake blonde wearing very low-cut flared jeans and a bikini top. She looks like a not-so-little mermaid, about seventeen going on thirty—but I can't really tell through her mask of makeup.

"Jazz Gomez," Geraldo says, looking at me in the rearview mirror. "The new singing sensation on the island."

"So famous no one over twenty, who has any sense, has heard of her," says Abuela through her hanky, which she is holding to her nose as if to say, *Anything Geraldo says about music stinks.*

"Anyone who keeps up with the music scene has heard of Jazz. Doris, her voice reminds me of yours."

"You are *loco* if you really believe that, Geraldo. Doris is a singer. This girl makes noises while a mixer plays background. It's her package they're selling. Look at that poor child, made up like a streetwalker. That's not glamour. It's trash with a little sparkle." My mother says all this with a smile on her face while looking at me.

"Yes, we know, Claribel. You are the glamorous star, everyone else is trashy." Geraldo gives my mother a disdainful look that makes me so angry I throw the CD over the seat. It hits him on the head, he slams on the brakes, and we all pitch forward.

"*¡Qué diablos!*" he shouts.

"I am so sorry, Geraldo," my grandmother says, taking the blame. "The thing just flew out of my hands. Maybe if you drive a little bit slower, we wouldn't have accidents."

She puts one finger over her lips when I start to say something. I see that she is still trying to let Geraldo hang himself in front of Mami. He's doing a good job as far as I can see.

San Juan is a huge city, and it looks like everyone is out driving. In comparison to the crazies we meet on the road, Geraldo begins to look like a very careful driver. People cut in front without warning, honk their horns nonstop, and pass in the emergency lanes. Maybe there is a daily quota of traffic accidents in the capital. The park is jam-packed, mainly with teenagers. Most of them are impersonating famous rappers, with nose rings, neon hair dyes, tons of fake gold neck chains and diamond rings, the works. The girls' costumes are modeled on the popular video-dancer look, three or four inches of microfiber stretched over the Latina curves. Suddenly, I am in familiar territory, although the landscape is very different from my own barrio neighborhood. This park overlooks the ocean. The water is turquoise. The surface actually glitters in the sun. It looks like a palm-tree-framed postcard. Except when a guy with low-hung cut-offs, green hair, and a bare chest showing a tattoo of a skull steps into my field of vision. Then the scene turns into a postcard you buy in a shop your *mamá* doesn't want you to go into. He gives me the once-over and laughs mockingly, as if I were a dog standing on its hind legs, or a monkey performing for the crowds at the zoo.

He points to my cocktail dress of black satin with gold trim and matching gold sandals. It's one of my mother's old nightclub costumes. It's strapless, so I thought it'd be cooler than what I really wanted to wear, a red skin-tight gown, floor length, with matching elbow-length red gloves. But Mami convinced me that I would die of heat prostration if I wore that today.

"*Vámonos.*" Abuela gives the kid one of her stares, the kind that can turn a person into a pile of dust. She takes Mami and me by the hand and leads us to the tent where we will wait to go onstage.

We share the tent with all the other opening acts. The first group is a trio whose average age must be a hundred years. They are practicing their harmonies. The other act is a magician. He's carrying a cage covered with a black cloth. I hear the familiar sounds of birds coming from his corner. I go over to investigate.

"Are they pigeons?" I ask the magician dressed in a tuxedo, speaking in my minimal but careful Spanish. He wipes his sweat-drenched face with a towel, smearing his stage makeup.

"*Palomas,*" he says. He lifts the cover, and I see two gray doves crouching in a cage too small for them. They are making sounds that sound like distress calls to me.

"Aren't they hot in there?"

He shrugs, covers the box, and turns away from me. The

show is about to start. It is sponsored by about fifteen products, from beer to soap, and the MC tries to make his pitches while the crowd shouts one name over and over: "Jazz, Jazz, Jazz."

I turn to find Geraldo right behind me.

"So where is the star?" I ask, trying not to sound as curious as I feel. Does she get her own tent, I wonder?

Geraldo takes me by the elbow and leads me outside. He points to a huge trailer parked right on the beach. There are policemen all around it.

"Right in that air-conditioned trailer. That's where Jazz will be, getting every single thing she asks for brought to her."

I say nothing. Geraldo whispers in my ear, "You do sing better than Jazz. And with a little makeup and the right clothes . . ."

I yank my arm away from his sweaty fingers and go back inside. I sit with my mother and grandmother as close as possible to the industrial-strength fans they have positioned around the stage. Even though I try not to focus on the doves, I hear the desperate flapping of their wings in their cramped quarters, and their cries for air, for water. I know what they need. I have learned the language of birds. It breaks my heart to know they are in pain, and I have to hold myself back when I see the magician leave the tent to smoke a cigarette. I have the strongest urge to go open the cage door and set the birds free. But I see that Mami is trying hard to get through this show, and I can't risk making trouble for her.

When we get the five-minute call, Abuela stands us up to

inspect us. Mami is thin, but she still looks like a movie star in her flowing green satin dress and matching satin high-heeled shoes. I am not as pretty as she is, but for once, I don't mind. Abuela looks over at us as if we were the finalists in the Miss Universe competition.

"*Hija*, you are *bellísima*. And you, Doris . . ." She turns me around, then spreads her arms dramatically, "*De tal palo, tal astilla.*"

I think that means something like I am a chip off the old block.

The crowd is still chanting "Jazz, Jazz" when it's time for us to go on. The combo has arrived at the last minute and begins to set up. To my horror, I hear some boos from the crowd. Mami smiles encouragingly at me. Abuela acts like our bodyguard, hovering, as if to protect us from invisible enemies. My stomach does a cartwheel as the MC announces the University Players and my mother's name as a vocalist. The crowd continues its chant of "Jazz, Jazz." I see the older musician, the professor, come up to my mother and kiss her hand. He is a dark-skinned man with beautiful silver hair. He is carrying a classical guitar as if it were made of glass. Her eyes open wide when she looks at him. Her face is radiant when she turns to me: "Doris, this is *el profesor* Ed Shomberg Sánchez. He teaches music at the university." She has to shout above the noise of the crowd. El Profesor makes as if to kiss my hand, too, but I pull away. It's showtime. And I am scared.

The MC yells an introduction into the microphone, and

we walk onstage. The "combo" is the professor on guitar, one guy on bongos, and another with maracas and a table behind him with a bunch of other stuff on it: a tambourine, a gourd, wood clappers. I cringe. Unless we have amplifiers the size of a garage, we'll never be heard.

There is a lull in the crowd noise as a helicopter passes overhead. We get the cue to start our number. But it's practically impossible to hear ourselves speak with everyone yelling. People must have decided that it's Jazz being brought in by helicopter, and they begin to shout her name again. My mother takes my hand and we keep singing. Police move in on horses to barricade the trailer and a sort of riot erupts. The professor shakes his head no. He takes my mother's hand, she holds on to mine, and we exit the stage. Abuela is pacing in the tent. The magician is yelling at the MC that he is going on no matter what. He grabs the caged doves and pushes past us onstage. The last thing I see before I am pulled toward the band's van is the magician opening the cage and grabbing one of the doves. The bird, apparently frightened by the noise of the crowd, pecks him. Startled, he lets it go, and the *paloma* flies off, followed by the other bird. Elated, I watch them rise above the screaming people and disappear among the palm trees. My mother looks up and exclaims, "How beautiful they are in flight!" And I shout, *"¡Si yo tuviera alas!"*

Recognizing her own favorite, often repeated wish, Mami laughs, but looks at me in a quizzical way, as if it had never occurred to her that I, too, sometimes wish *I* had wings.

* * *

El Profesor drives us expertly out of the park, maneuvering among the police cars pulling in as the helicopter attempts to land.

Abuela keeps muttering ¡*Ay bendito!* and adjusting her seat belt. My mother sits between us, breathing too rapidly. I'm afraid that she will have a heart attack. El Profesor pulls into a parking lot on the university's campus.

"*Bueno, muchachos.* I'll leave you here. Thank you. We will talk later."

The two young men take their instruments and wave goodbye. It's all happening too fast.

Then we drive to a restaurant in Old San Juan. It's as if we've gone back to Spanish times, when Ponce de León was governor. The streets are made of cobblestone and the buildings are very old. El Profesor greets the waiter as if he knows him. We get a table outside on the patio. Palm trees are swaying softly in the breeze from the nearby ocean.

And as we are served *café con leche*, sweet as chocolate, I see that the professor is leaning over to speak to my mother. She is fanning herself with a painted Spanish fan my *abuela* had brought out of her purse. Her cheeks have color again.

"How are you feeling, Claribel?"

"I will be fine, Eduardo," she says, but I see that she is lying. There's a flush on her skin, as if from a fever. Her whole body is visibly trembling.

"I think we need to go home as soon as possible," my grandmother says.

"Señora, I agree with you." The professor is now holding my mother's hand and patting it. Who does this guy think he is, anyway? She is letting him make a lot of decisions, and I resent it, even if they are the right ones.

"If you will permit me, I will drive you to your pueblo."

"What about Geraldo?" I ask, not that I care. I just want to see Mami's reaction. I last saw him circling the trailer. I hope he's gotten arrested for trespassing.

My grandmother makes as if she's washing her hands. "That one? *Se quedó sin la soga y sin la cabra.*" Okay, so Geraldo has been left with neither the rope nor the goat. I accept Abuela's sentencing, and we take off down the narrow alleys of the ancient Spanish town, out of the big city and back on the highway. My mother keeps her eyes closed the whole trip. When we arrive home, El Profesor puts his arm around her waist because she seems too weak to walk by herself. Then, suddenly, she lets out a high-pitched cry, almost like she's trying to hit the highest note on the scales, and collapses in his arms.

They have her back in the van before I can open my mouth. Abuela yells out the window as they pull out of her steep driveway, causing cars to screech to a halt in the narrow street. "I will call you, Doris. Wait here."

For what seems an eternity, I sit by the phone and wait. I get up and go around the house. It is hot, so hot I feel I am suffocating. I open windows so I can hear the phone, and I go to the backyard and sit under Abuela's grapefruit tree. It is cooler there, but there are bees circling around my head like they want to say something but cannot get it out. I go back into my room and lie down. I read a little in the book of dreams that Doña Iris gave me before I fall asleep. It is rare to dream of the mother as she appears in real life, unless she is gone or has died, and then it is a memory, the book says. Most times the mother appears in dreams as a symbol. For example, a flowering plant or tree in a dream may symbolize the caring mother, while a desert or a dry well, dead or dying nature, may stand for the distant or cruel maternal figure.

I wake up from a dark dream that I cannot bring back no matter how hard I try. I am scared and angry. Why hadn't they waited for me? I should be there with my mother. What if she's dying at this very moment? Wouldn't she ask for me, her only child? I do something then that I have not done in years. I slip down out of the tall bed onto the cool tile floor, on my knees. And I pray.

I make promises and deals with anyone Up There who may be listening. The hard floor hurts my knees after a while, but I make myself stay on my knees for a long time. Mainly I repeat over and over, "Let her be all right. Let her be all right."

The phone rings and I get up in a panic. They will be home soon, Abuela announces, and before I can ask any questions, she hangs up.

It seems like years before the car pulls into the driveway, and the professor and Abuela escort Mami into the house. Abuela takes over and leads her slowly to her room. I hear the window AC switch on. Then, as I listen to Abuela, a whirlwind of activity, making my mother comfortable, I sit motionless in the living room, not saying a word. El Profesor asks me the usual questions: what grade am I in, where do I go to school. He regrets not getting to hear me sing. Another time, perhaps? He tells me that he is a musicologist at the University of Puerto Rico. The combo is part of a project to lead a revival of the old music on the island. "Today was a disaster, but it was a mistake to combine the program, to try to have a public that would appreciate the traditional *canciones* and this trendy rap music. But it is not always like this," he tells me. "With the right audience, our programs are very successful." He seems to be talking to himself mainly, his eyes darting to Mami's bedroom and back to me. He is speaking and I am pretending to listen. But we are both just waiting. Waiting to hear that Mami is okay.

Finally, Abuela comes out of the bedroom.

"*Profesor, mil gracias* for taking us to the emergency room. I have called her doctor, and he agrees she should rest now. But tomorrow, she will have to go in to see him."

"I will call Claribel tomorrow, if you permit me, señora. Doris, it was a pleasure to meet you." He bows his head in my direction but does not try to kiss my hand. I am dizzy from the day. I wish I were home and could run up to the roof. Doña Iris would be there to tell me more about what my dreams mean, and to wait for Martha to appear on the horizon. She and I always stood up as Martha got nearer, to let her see us and to wave her in. Sometimes, Martha would make circles over the roof, while the other birds came into sight. It was not until they all alighted that she would allow us to stroke her feathers. No matter how bad a day I'd had, this little homecoming ceremony always made me feel calm. On the roof, I always felt I could think things through. Today my chest is tight with fear, and I am homesick for familiar things and people.

"Is Mami going to be okay, Abuela?" The cocktail dress I'm still wearing is sticking to me. She sees me trying to unzip it and helps me get out of it. Her hands are strong for an old lady's. She and Mami are a lot alike, tiny women with hands like steel.

"Doris, your mother is never going to be like she was. She has to realize this herself and slow down. Nobody can make her do it."

"What about El Profesor?" I ask a little sarcastically.

"He is a nice man. A widower. Your mother likes him, *mucho*."

"I noticed."

"He is worth a thousand Geraldos."

"Only a thousand?"

"Maybe more, but I don't like to put people down, *hija*."

I laugh in spite of myself.

"I need to lie down," I say. I am tired, but mainly I'm lonely. Lonely for my friends, weird old Yolanda and crazy Arturo. I even wish I could call Danny. He was always good for a squeeze or two. And where is my father? Too busy with his bands and his girlfriend to care what happens to me. Or to Mami.

"I have turned the fans on already. I will bring you milk and *un sándwich de jamón y queso. ¿Está bien?*"

"Abuela, I'm not hungry."

"You will be. And you don't want your stomach to wake you up in the middle of the night. I'm going to check on your mother. Then I will be back."

I sigh in resignation. Abuela is a compulsive nurturer. I can see why Mami comes back to her when she needs to heal. I wish Mami were more like her mother. But then Abuela is not a fabulous singer with a bad heart. But no matter what I tell myself about my mother's *special needs*, that empty feeling starts making a hole in my chest again.

I peek into Mami's room on my way to mine. She appears to be sleeping. Abuela has put a glass of water on her bedside table. A ceiling fan is turning slowly, making the curtains rise and fall gently; the AC is humming; and the *coquís* are beginning their evening song just outside her window. It seems like Mami has everything she needs right here.

13

The phone rings for a long time before I realize that no one is going to get it. I see the note on the phone stand in Abuela's fancy handwriting: "Gone to the doctor."

"Hello?" I am out of breath from jumping out of sleep so suddenly.

"Are you okay, Doris?" my father asks.

"I'm fine, Papi. What's up?"

"Doris, it's good to hear your voice. It feels like you've been away longer than a few days. We miss you, *hija*."

"Papi, she's really sick," I say to him just like that.

"I know, Doris. I talked to your *abuela* already. I called because I thought you'd like to know about Yolanda."

"What about her?"

"Perez. Remember the police officer who, uh . . . interviewed us?"

"I remember Perez," I say.

"Perez says that Kenny's mom refused to press charges against her. She's . . . uh . . ."

"She's pregnant, Papi. The word is *pregnant*. It's Kenny's baby, that's why she won't press charges."

Silence. I actually hear him swallow hard. I'm willing to bet that he's thinking about me doing the same thing as Yoli, getting myself "in trouble," as he and Mami still call it. Predictable old Papi. I guess he knows a thing or two about getting in trouble.

"Anyway, Doris. Because Kenny's mom isn't pressing charges, Perez has convinced the district attorney to send Yolanda to a residence for teen mothers instead of jail until the . . . uh . . . baby is born. She'll have to meet with a parole officer after that."

"So that's lucky for Yoli," I say. "It could have been much worse."

"That's true," Papi says.

"So what if I decide not to come back?" I ask, changing the subject.

There is a long silence, but I can hear Papi doing that deep sighing that means he is struggling for answers. I know he is trying to think of what he should say to me at this moment. I wait. I want him to say it.

"Doris?"

"Papi?"

"I think you should come home as we planned."

"Why, Papi?"

"I made a special omelet for breakfast today, you know, with avocados and onions and all. Well . . . I accidentally put three plates on the table. I miss you, *hija*."

"Are you lying to me?"

"About making the *tortilla* with onions? Just joking. No. Doris, both your mami and I think it is better for you to come home after your visit. It's not the same here without you."

"She needs me now."

"She has your *abuela*. They have each other."

"Papi, you have Margarita. I'm just in the way there." Then, to my surprise, I hear myself saying, with a lump the size of an avocado in my throat, "I think I'm in the way here, too."

He waits a few heartbeats before he speaks again.

"I love your mother, Doris. I always will. But not like I love you. You are my family, Doris. Just before I called you, I was sitting here thinking about how you took over those birds after Don Pichón died. I didn't keep my word to him; you kept it for me. I've been going up there, I even let Doña Iris read my palm."

"What did she say?"

"She said someone that you love is far away and getting farther, getting ready to spread her wings and fly."

There is a moment of silence between us. What can anyone say after one of Doña Iris's pronouncements?

"Papi, what should I do?"

"You have always been the one with the plan, Doris."

"I don't know what to do. She's sick. Papi, I'm scared."

There is silence again. I can practically hear him thinking. He knows this is important to me, and he's got to choose his words carefully. Then he says exactly what I need him to say at this moment.

"I love you, Doris. I forgot to tell you that before you left."

"Say hello to Margarita for me, Papi." I say this to thank him for his words, and to my surprise, I find that I am not angry when I think of her. In fact, I am sort of grateful that she's with Papi while I'm away.

"I'll tell Margarita that you will be home soon. I mean . . ."

"I love you, Papi."

After I get dressed, I sit on the porch, in Abuela's rocker, to wait for them to get home. Some little girls are playing jump rope on the sidewalk, and they sing to keep time:

¡Que llueva!
¡Que llueva!
Los pajaritos cantan,
las nubes se levantan.

Let it rain, let it rain, the little birds are singing, the clouds are lifting. In the distance I can see the green mountains that divide the island in two: rain clouds are moving in our direction, bringing a cooling breeze with them. It seems like every day, around the same time in the afternoon, we get drenched with a quick downpour. Afterward, everything looks greener and cleaner. I don't know exactly why, but I feel peaceful at last.

¡Que llueva! ¡Que llueva! Funny how all the real poetry of

a song is lost when you translate it, but the mystery of the words sometimes remains. I am glad I understand Spanish, even though I don't speak it too well. Mami is right. The old songs, even the silly children's rhymes, are like magic spells. Singing them changes the way you feel. Already I'm imagining saying *adiós*, or the less final *hasta luego*, to this beautiful, confusing place that Mami finds irresistible.

Suddenly, there is a commotion on the street that shatters my *momento de paz*. Two cars are facing each other head-on, their horns blaring, inching forward, like bulls about to face off in mortal combat. They can't both fit on the road, and neither driver will back up. Their shouts drown out the girls' song. The church bells start ringing the hour, and I hear loudspeakers on top of a huge van announcing a sale at the mall. I also see my grandmother's orange Toyota making its way up the street. Her horn joins the others in a crazy symphony of sound. Finally one of the two cars blocking the street gives in, and pulls into someone's driveway. This, of course, results in angry shouts and gestures from the homeowner whose territory has been violated. Just another day in paradise.

Abuela pulls into our carport muttering something I definitely will not try to translate—it would lose all its poetry.

"It's tachycardia," my mother announces, kicking off her high-heeled sandals. She may be sick, but she dresses like a star, even at seven a.m. and to visit the doctor. Her parrot-green sundress looks good on her new skinny body. Only the purple circles under her eyes and how carefully she is standing up and sitting down give away how bad she must feel.

"Takee-kardee-ah," Abuela repeats, shaking her head. Mami cracks up at her mother's tragic look. She takes Abuela's hands and pulls herself up to her feet. Then she leads her mother in a slow dance around the room.

"Ta-kee, ta-kee," she sings out, "takee-kardeeah *para mí*. Takee-kardeeah *para ti*. Tachycardia for me, and tachycardia for you. Tachycardia is what makes my heart beat fast. How about yours?"

Abuela is laughing so hard that tears run down her cheeks.

Suddenly Mami drops down next to me. She is out of breath, and exhausted by the impromptu performance of her tachycardia salsa song. She looks like a little girl in her bare feet, laughing. I catch her glancing at me, to see if I'm laughing, too. I am laughing at first, out of relief at seeing her alive, but then I look at Abuela, who looks tired, like she has taken a tour of hell in high heels.

"What does it mean?" I ask.

"It's an electrical problem," Mami says, winking at me. "I have bad wiring."

"Stop making jokes now, Claribel. Doris wants to know what's the matter with your heart. Tell her." Abuela has gone serious. She sits down across from us.

"Doris, I'm only half kidding. I have a congenital problem called heart block. It causes a problem with the transmission of electrical impulses between the two ventricles of my heart. That's why I faint sometimes, and why I get dizzy. It either beats too fast or too slow."

"How will they fix it?"

"Surgery is too risky right now since they have not located

all the places where my heart is blocked. If they can operate someday, I will have to get a pacemaker."

"So what are you going to do?" I am afraid that she is telling me that nothing is going to cure her.

"*El doctor* says that your mother has to change her life while they try to get her strong enough for exploratory surgery. She can't sing her heart out until they find a way to fix it."

"Seriously, what does he mean by *change her life?*"

"It just means no more San Juan riot concerts or facing San Juan *tapones* for me." She laughs again. *Tapón* is slang for traffic jam. Or maybe she's thinking of her stopped-up heart valves.

"Does this mean no gigs?"

"No," Mami says. "It means I have to get out of the contract I foolishly signed with Geraldo. I talked to the doctor about my work with the university combo. He didn't see any problem with that as long as I . . ."

"As long as she does not get too *excitada* like she does when she's onstage," Abuela interrupts. "That means no acting like a *loca* when she sings, no dancing all night. *¡Nada de eso!*"

"*Nada, nada, nada.* Takee-kardeeah means *nada para mí, nada para ti,*" Mami sings, blowing Abuela a kiss across the room.

"For a sick woman you are acting *muy feliz, hija.*" Abuela is obviously done with this conversation. She makes her hand-washing gesture, meaning *I am not listening to your foolish talk any longer.* "Your *mami* thinks she knows everything. *Pero, más sabe el diablo por viejo que por diablo.*"

"Huh?" This proverb leaves me blank. Abuela notes that my eyebrows have turned to question marks, and translates her wisdom for me. "The devil is wise because he's old, not because he's the devil, I always say."

"Oh," both of us say at once.

"I am going to make breakfast." Abuela leaves the room as we dissolve into giggles.

As soon as we're alone, my mother laughs, and says, "Your *abuela* just admitted to being the devil." She's still trying to keep things light, but I decide that now is the time for us to talk about the future.

"Mami, are you *ever* coming home?"

"Doris, *ever* is a word I can't say right now, you understand?" She takes my hands in hers. I feel the trembling. I think of her faulty wiring, how her lights go on and off like they do in this house right before a storm. I am thinking of storms because the day is turning dark. The clouds are moving in from the mountains. The little girls' jump-rope spell has called the rain.

"Papi called. He thinks I should go home after a few weeks. And I agree. My life is there, my school, my friends are there . . ." I can think of many reasons to go home now that I have started a list.

"I know your *papi* misses you already. I was real scared for you when I heard about the trouble with Arturo, Yolanda, and that crazy Matoa boy, Doris. That's why I called you to come be with me. And I'm so glad you did, *hija*. But it's obvious you can take care of yourself. You always have."

I look straight at her.

"I still need you, Mami."

"I know you do, but not as much as you think. And have you noticed something about mothers while you've been here with your *abuela* and me?"

"What? That mothers never stop bossing you around?"

"Yeah, that, too. But what I mean is that I came here, to my mother's house, because I need her now. She's the one person who can and will take care of me when I'm sick."

"We'll take care of you."

"*Mi amor*, who do you mean by *we*? You have to face the fact that your father has a new life now. Even before I knew I was sick, he and I had stopped being a couple. It's not that we don't care about each other. We just grew apart, you know? Finally, I had to leave. I'm sorry I didn't say goodbye properly. I wasn't planning to stay away so long, just long enough to think things through. That's why I left most of my things there. But now I know this is where I want to be."

She puts her hand on my shoulder and faces me. She has to look up into my eyes. I guess I have grown a little more in the past few months.

"We both love you, *hija*. But when you get really sick, things look different. I was scared, Doris. Scared that I would not get to do what I always wanted to do before I died."

"You don't seem scared now."

"I'm okay with it because at least I'm now singing *mi propia canción*, Doris. Even if I can't tour like I used to, singing is the one thing in my life I know I do well."

I have my own little electrical storm brewing in my head

and chest. Mami is talking to me as if I am her best friend, her equal, and I like it, but I really want her to feel sorry for me, too, to say she hates sending me away and regrets having left us. But, instead, she's calmly explaining why she had to disappear, and why she won't be returning home.

She seems to know what I'm feeling, because she pulls my head to her chest like she used to do when I was little, telling me to feel her voice singing to me through the vibrations the music made inside her. It was as though she had a harp in her chest.

"You are my *cielito lindo*."

"That's good to know." I can't help sounding a little sarcastic. I know she loves me, in her own way. I give her hand a little squeeze so she knows we're okay. Then I help her to her feet. Time to get on with our crazy life. Our *vida loca*.

"I made an elegant breakfast right out of the pages of *Buenhogar* magazine for you, *mis niñas*." Abuela waves us into the kitchen. "Come look, so healthy. Mango slices with low-fat cream, homemade bread, fresh-squeezed grapefruit juice, and *café con leche*. Sit down and eat. *Buen provecho*."

"It's beautiful, Mamá," Mami says, giving me a slight wink. "But I really was hoping for a three-egg-and-onion tortilla deep-fried in Crisco." I sit on the chair facing the window. There is a rumble of thunder and rain starts falling, but the sun is still shining.

Abuela opens her mouth to speak, but Mami and I look at each other, and beat her to it.

"*El diablo* is beating his wife!"

* * *

That night I dream of snow. Our barrio is covered with a beautiful layer of pure white. I am playing in the street with Arturo, who is making snow angels, flapping his arms like a bird on the soft piles of snow. I wake up confused. For a moment, I think I'm back in my old room. Then I hear a *coquí*'s song and the whirring of the fan over me. I am homesick.

14

For the rest of my visit, I focus on really seeing things, like Doña Iris taught me. I learn from Abuela how to make candy from mangoes, how to tell if an avocado is ripe enough to spread like butter on hot bread, how to eavesdrop on interesting conversations while I wait and wait in line at the bank, at the stores, at the beauty shop. No one seems to be in a real hurry here, and even if you are, nobody else hurries on your account, so you might as well deal with it.

Mami says that time is a cultural thing, and that she has her internal clock set on Puerto Rican Standard Time.

Maybe that's why your heart beats erratically, I tell her. Puerto Rican timekeeping is not regulated by any law, natural or man-made. I also see that if Mami starts to feel faint, Abuela is right there to help her to a chair, to demand a glass of cold water for her, to make her go home and lie down if Abuela thinks it's necessary. And I realize that Mami enjoys having her mother fuss over her.

One night the three of us are watching television. It's a

live variety show featuring all the hot new island singers. Jazz is being interviewed. Mami and I are laughing hysterically at her obvious ignorance. She knows *nada, nada, nada* about music. The killer is that when she finally gets up to perform, and is obviously lip-syncing—she even forgets the words to the song! She never catches on. Luckily, the camera shifts to her hips and butt and stays there. Suddenly, the three of us hear clapping. It's Geraldo, blocking the doorway. He comes in without a word and lays down some important-looking papers on the coffee table in front of Mami.

"What is it, Geraldo?" Abuela asks in an irritated tone. "Can't you see we are watching quality programming?"

"It's a contract for Doris."

"*¿Qué dices, diablo?*" My grandmother is on her feet and hovering over him like an eagle about to pounce on a rabbit.

"Listen before you go hysterical, señora. She"—he points to my mother, curled up on the sofa (she's had one of her bad days)—"cannot fulfill the remaining dates on her calendar. But Doris can. You told me she can sing even better than you, Claribel. I'm gonna trust you on this." He is sounding a little desperate. He must really be out of options in his search for a young Latina who can at least pretend to sing. "I've got her opening up for Jazz next Saturday. Doris, what do you say? Wanna be a Caribbean queen like Jazz? Whaddya say?"

He has slipped into his Nuyorican cool-dude mode for my benefit. It's as fake as he is, since he's really a New Jerseyrican, born and bred in the Garden State, just like I was. But he's such a funny-looking guy in his tight black pants and tacky shirt with a Puerto Rican flag design and a big white star over his heart that I kind of feel sorry for him.

"She's a minor, Señor Demonio," Abuela says, "and we have doctor's orders on Claribel. Your contract is a pile of horse dung."

Geraldo ignores Abuela. He extends his arms out to me as if expecting me to fall into them.

"Doris, whaddya say, *mi amor*? I talked to a lawyer. There's a thing called the emancipated minor law, where you declare your independence from Mami and Papi. With your talent, there'll be no trouble convincing a judge."

"Will I get to sing any song I want, Geraldo?" I go over to sit by Mami. Abuela is already there, standing guard over her, arms crossed over her chest. In Doña Iris's book on reading gestures, there is a caption under a picture of a man sitting just like that. It is called "The Rock of Gibraltar." It means, "Go ahead, fool, make my day." Poor Geraldo doesn't know my grandmother is loading the word-weapons she will soon discharge on him.

"New songs, Doris, you can sing the new songs. The ones you hear on the radio. A girl your age ought to be glad to get a chance . . ."

I whisper in Mami's ear and we both start singing "Bésame Mucho" at the top of our lungs.

Even Abuela joins in. She tears through our harmonizing like a bulldozer. My mother and I did not inherit our singing voices from her, that's for sure.

171

Geraldo gives us the evil eye. Then he picks up his papers from the table.

"*¡Tres mujeres estúpidas!*" he shouts, turning on the heels of his shiny black shoes.

"Sounds like a good title for a Jazz number to me," my mother calls after him.

He takes off in such a hurry that he scratches the front bumper of his rented sports car on the curb. We repeat the refrain of "Bésame Mucho" until we drown out his curses.

"*Bueno, pájaro que comió, pájaro que voló,*" says Abuela, looking out the window at the tire marks left on her driveway from Geraldo's dramatic exit.

"So the bird eats his fill, then flies away," my mother says, translating Abuela's cryptic pronouncement about Geraldo.

"I hope that bird can digest all the junk he eats off the streets, *hija*. Doris, are you sure you don't want to be the next Jazz, the Caribbean queen?"

"Maybe when I grow me some hips like hers, Abuela."

On the television there is a shot of the star leaving the studio surrounded by hundreds of screaming fans, all shouting her name. For a moment, I wonder whether I could have had a chance at fame here. But only for a moment. Geraldo is wrong. We are not three stupid women. We are not stupid at all.

Mami is falling asleep on my shoulder. All the medicines she's taking make her groggy. I gently lay her head down on my lap. I put my hand lightly on her chest where her heart is beating as fast as a bird's. I can feel it slowing down to almost normal as she relaxes into her dreams.

Before I go to my room, I fold the piece of notepaper with a poem I've written for her into a bird shape, a bird with outspread wings, and place it gently on her chest, over her heart.

A Poem for Mami

Quick, kiss me, *bésame mucho.* Break this spell.
When I return to my true shape, I am a bird
called the Thief of Love. I bring you gifts from where
    I've been.
You have my heart, but we are different. Don't cry,
    the rain will stop.
And when it does, I'll have to fly away.
I will be dreaming of Puerto Rico, but I have my
    songs,
and you have yours. And you have the rain every
    afternoon,
bringing the cool breezes, turning everything green
    again.
And you have me, circling home, a bit of gold in my
    beak.
I am still me, with wings.
No longer trapped in a spell. I am the bird
that flies away, but will return. You know the songs
that will bring me home.
Muchos besos de tu hija.
Tu cielito lindo.

Part Four

Pigeons . . . learn to recognise their young as individuals about fledging time.

15

Arturo and I go visit Yolanda just after school starts. She is looking very pregnant, even in the shapeless blue jumpsuit that all the girls have to wear at the residence.

"I'm gonna name him Huracán if it's a boy. Whaddya think?"

"Is the baby's father going to give him his notorious last name, Yoli?" Arturo asks.

"Huracán is his baby, and he's gonna carry his name. Huracán Matoa. Name sounds strong. Like he's gonna be," says Yolanda, flipping through a coloring book called *The Taino Indians of Puerto Rico*. She is taking a course where you have to research your ethnic background. "Look, guys, doesn't she look like me?" She hands the coloring book to Arturo. "I think one of my ancestors was probably an Indian princess." She shows us an illustration in the book with a caption: "Guanina, a Taino chief's sister, was the wife of a conquistador. She became a hero when she warned her brother's tribe that the Spaniards were coming to attack their village."

"The Spanish were criminals," Yolanda says, "they *exterminated* all my people."

"You are probably part Spanish, too, Yoli. Like Doris and me, an attractive blend of Spanish, Indian, and African. Because we, the not-so-completely-*exterminated* people of the Caribbean, are mestizos, a mixed race, and proud of it, too." Arturo laughs. He has already started coloring the illustration. He makes Guanina's face one third brown, one third black, and one third pink.

"Hey!" Yolanda grabs the book away.

"So what do you *do* here, Yoli?" I suddenly feel like I'm a lot older than they are. Even though Yolanda is going to have a baby and has shot a man, she still acts like a kid. Arturo *is* a little more mature, but he's still into games, always playing a part, like he hasn't decided who or what he is yet.

"We go to classes, all-girl classes." Yolanda makes a face at this. "We all have jobs around the place in the afternoon, cooking, laundry, cleaning. Then after dinner we watch movies on parenting and child care. Once a week we volunteer at a day-care center, to get real-life experience with kids, you know."

"Do you like it?" I am honestly curious. Yolanda looks calmer than I have seen her since her father died. But then, maybe her "condition" is making her act different. I hear those maternal hormones take over a woman's body like an invading army.

She doesn't answer right away. It's like she hadn't considered the question before.

"I like having something to do, you know, every hour. It makes me feel, I don't know . . ."

"Secure?" Arturo volunteers. He looks a little sad. Security is one thing he hasn't had in his life.

"I guess that's it. I don't have to think about anything here. I have three outfits. I'm wearing one of them, and the other two in my closet look just like it."

"It's pretty ugly, Yoli," Arturo says in a sweet voice.

"Nobody's here to see me, except other fat girls, who are not exactly supermodels themselves."

"Have you heard from Kenny?" I ask. I had heard he was still in bad shape and had to be under medical supervision for a long time.

"He's in P.S. 22."

"The alternative school, right?"

"Yeah. He calls me sometimes."

"What for?" I can hardly believe that Yolanda could take up with a thug like Kenny Matoa, shoot him, then talk on the phone with him.

"He's my baby's *papi*, Doris! He wants to know how we are. I don't think you understand what real love is."

I have to resist firing off a few questions about several crucial things I don't understand about Yolanda and Kenny's kind of *love*. For example, having a baby without thinking how they're going to support it is a strange way to be a loving person. But I decide she has enough problems without me forcing her to face the facts of her *vida loca*, her crazy life that is about to change. But she'll have a *real* reality check when she has the baby and has to leave this place.

"Does your mother come see you, Yoli?" Arturo asks. "I see her at the supermarket sometimes."

"Yeah. But she hates Kenny, so it's a problem, you know. I told her she better get used to him. We're gonna be together for our baby. Maybe get married, too."

I decide to exit on that late-breaking news flash.

"Come on, Arturo, we have to go over the script for tomorrow."

"Okay," says Arturo. He goes over to Yolanda and hugs her, being careful not to press too hard on her volley-ball-size belly. "Yoli, Huracán was the Taino god of thunder and war, right? That name will let everyone know to take cover when they see him coming down the street. El Huracán is on the way!"

Yolanda smiles and puts both hands on her stomach. "Yeah. He's gonna be a cool kid."

16

Only three pigeons, besides Martha and her two hatchlings, are left in the condo. They are not in great shape. We don't really know where the others have gone or whether they'll be back. Papi admitted that he didn't check on them every day, and Doña Iris can't remember whether she's been feeding them regularly, so that may be the problem. I noticed when I got home that her mind was wandering more than usual. She talks to Don Pichón all the time. The cages are filthy. The floor is covered with droppings as hard as concrete. Martha seems jumpy and will not let us near her nestlings.

I get up early and go to the roof almost every day. I am taking the condo apart and building one open loft for Martha, her family, and the last of her troops. The birds themselves will decide whether they want to stay.

Margarita and my father sleep late after playing at the Caribbean Moon, but she still insists on leaving me food in the oven for the next day. She's a deadly combination of Jewish and Puerto Rican mother. She must figure that if she can get me to eat, we can work anything out.

I go over my lines in *West Side Story Revisited*, the play we will put on under Ms. Torres's direction. We bring in our re-writes every day of rehearsal. If Ms. Torres thinks a scene is working well, she retypes the pages and makes copies for the cast. It's so cool. We're writing this play as we act out our roles, creating our own version of the characters. I am María—the meanest María there ever was on a stage. Arturo is Tony. My own twist to the story is that María is not interested in Tony and the feeling is mutual. But then, the love issues take a back seat in our version. María gets the girls together to rumble against the boys. We decide to use our voices and face off in a sort of musical slam, boys on one side, girls on the other. We compete to come up with the best rants.

"Hey, hey, Tony, whaddya say? Can you *papis* come out and play? Show us what you got, or are you wimping out?" The girls shout a challenge toward the dark part of the stage.

"María, María, you can shout. But are you *mamis* ready to hang out?" The boys, led by Tony, come onstage, menacing us with their body language, and they keep coming toward us making some dance moves, but we hold our ground. "Are you ready to hang out with Mighty Tony?"

We go at it with words and extemporized rumble dance steps for a while, then we break out, rapping or singing or speaking our monologues one by one, and then we do some more rumble dancing (we haven't worked out the choreography yet). We have many ideas, and it's a little chaotic, but everyone is getting her or his moment in the spotlight. Ms. T. has asked each of us to showcase our individual talents. That means that we have ended up with a sort of *West Side Story* meets *A Chorus Line*.

Every day the script changes, and it's a new play. The extemporizing is fun, and I get to sing a little, too. My voice sounds better than it ever has. Ms. T. even says maybe I should take private voice lessons so I can apply for a college scholarship. But even though I'm still not sure that this is what I want, when I'm in the middle of a scene, or dancing up a storm, I feel right. I feel like I'm near where I want to be. And this sense of things being right is unusual for Doris, the Problem Queen of *El Barrio*. I think this play is letting me find my real voice, and every day I hear it clearer and clearer. Like Doña Iris says, you have to find your gift and accept it. I can sing, and I can sing whatever song I want.

"How was the Russian bread I baked for you yesterday?" Margarita sings out to me from the kitchen door. She has dragged herself out of bed to get praise for her food even though she's had barely two hours of sleep.

"Good. I was just leaving for school." I grab my backpack and head for the door, but she blocks me.

"Here, take the rest of it for a snack. You got lunch money?"

"Yeah. See you. I'll be late. Play rehearsal." Margarita is really taking this domestic thing a little bit too seriously. I think she's practicing to be my loving stepmother (isn't this a contradiction in terms? I ask myself). Papi loves all the smothering, but I am used to a more, shall we say, *detached* sort of mother-daughter thing. But I give Margarita a friendly wave as I grab a slice of the bread and leave. I don't want to discourage her too much. I mean I *could* get used to coming home to a hot meal and a smile across the table.

Mami. The thought of her makes me stop at the top of the stairs. My mother's face is not as clear in my mind as it used to be, though it's only a couple of months since I saw her. I can hear her voice. I remember things she said word for word, but her face and the little details, you know, like the color of her favorite lipstick, the smell of her perfume, are now harder for me to remember. I take my compact out of my purse and look at myself. I call her into the mirror, same color of skin, eyes the shape of almonds, full lips (made for kissing, she always says), but everything comes together different on her face. She is beautiful and I'm not. I have a few good points of my own, and I'm making the best of them, but I'll never be beautiful like her. For one, I am letting my bird's nest hair grow out for the play, and it's looking good and big. Big, crazy hair. My María is a wild girl.

At school everything and nothing is the same. I mean, the teachers don't change. They're still wearing the same boring clothes, saying the same boring things. But *I* have changed. My hope of a reconciliation between my parents is gone, and I am slowly beginning to realize that I need to let go, subtract some people from the equation. It seems like it's a matter of doing the simple math: add this person, subtract that one.

It was harder than I had thought it would be leaving Mami at Abuela's. Every time the phone rings, I think it's about

Mami's heart condition. Papi is still Papi, still totally involved in managing the bands. And now that Margarita is living with us, he doesn't have to worry about little things, like food or making sure everything doesn't go to pieces around him. I am beginning to understand why a woman like Mami would start getting restless after fifteen years with him. Don't get me wrong, my father is not a loser. He's just not a liberated guy. He's old-style Latino-macho in some ways. He still needs a good little woman, or in Ms. M.'s case, a good *big* woman, to keep him out of trouble. But I wonder, does he need me more than I need him?

For instance, just last night, before he and Margarita left for the club, he asked me if I'd done anything new to my hair.

"I'm letting it grow."

"Your mom had beautiful long hair like that when I first saw her . . ." Then he looks sad, like he's lost in the old memories of my mother's beautiful long hair, which, if it really looked like my semi-Afro does now, must have been a wild sight. Can't account for a man's taste. I note that Papi is talking about Mami in the past tense these days, when he talks about her at all.

"Thanks, Papi. Mami says she's letting her hair grow out again, too." I don't think he hears me. He gets quiet before he looks me in the eyes again.

"Doris?"

I wait for him to say something. But whatever it is, he has swallowed it.

Instead he smiles and says, "Your hair looks good that way."

"I'm happy to know you approve, Papi."

"Know your character's motivation" is Ms. Torres's new motto. She keeps asking the players, "What's your motivation?" She went back to L.A. last summer and took directing classes at a Method actor's school. So now she wants us to "live, love, and suffer" for our characters, "rejoice" for them, "become" them. No problem: all the kids in the play know a little about suffering, and being Latinos, we can "rejoice" on demand. I've been thinking about motivation. Ms. T. told us that once you know what makes your character tick, you can act. I figure it's the same with real people. If you can find out what makes them do what they do, it's easier to make room for them in your life. I am trying to get to Papi's motivation; then I'll try to decipher Margarita's. I think I've got Mami's figured out pretty well. And Abuela is an open book, every chapter its own wise saying.

Out on our street, I notice for the first time how well-behaved the drivers are here in comparison to Puerto Rican islanders, especially the residents of the beautiful, ancient capital of San Juan. Nobody is threatening anybody's life with a two-thousand-pound vehicle here. Of course, the street is wide enough to fit two lanes of cars at once, which helps.

I see that there are women lining up in front of the bodega already. Once a week a truck comes in from Miami with goodies from the island. Limited supply, though. Gotta fight for your island coffee and your refrigerated *pasteles* made by some old *abuela* on the island. The record shop is blaring its salsa music, a merengue from the Dominican Republic. I can't help shaking my booty to it. That's when Arturo sneaks up on me and takes me in his arms like a ballroom dancer, and we do one mean merengue right there in front of the eight o'clock crowd. Some of the women at the bodega cheer us on. It's never too early in the morning to do some "rejoicing" around here.

Then Arturo, who cannot resist an audience, regales everyone with his own rendition of "I Just Met a Girl Named María." There is a scattering of applause. "This one is a *papi chulo*," says one of the women, and they laugh, agreeing that he is a Puerto Rican dreamboat.

"*Gracias. Gracias.*" He blows kisses to his adoring, now quickly dispersing fans as the bodega opens, and I drag him down the street to school. Nothing like a little show of public affection to put Arturo in an excellent mood.

"*Muy bien.* It's showtime," Ms. Torres sings out.

The girls and the guys take their places on opposite sides of the stage, facing off.

The curtain rises to a small crowd of loyal parents (including Papi and Margarita), teachers, and a lot of loud students, both Latino and mainstream.

Ms. T. clicks on the taped music of a salsa version of "When You're a Jet." Everyone jumps onstage and we begin our individual dances. Throughout the play, Ms. T. is backstage, directing us frantically in stage whispers and wild hand gestures to spread ourselves out. Somehow we make it to the last number, and there has been applause after each one!

The final rumble dance number is fantastic. Everyone, including the jocks, knows a little of some sort of dancing, and we each just do our thing, with a spotlight going from dancer to dancer, so everyone gets their minute and a half of fame.

The music fades and we walk toward our dance partners in the middle of two spotlights. Then . . . the music blares out again and everyone jumps in for the finale. Ms. T. thinks we should drop the curtain while the audience is still clapping.

During the final bow, a rose lands at my feet. As I pick it up, I see that Margarita is holding the rest of the bouquet, while my *papi* pitches another at me. He's smiling like crazy and trying hard to catch a glimpse of me. He has exerted himself so much in his excitement to cheer me on that I am sure he will need a neck-and-arm rub with Bengay tonight. I may just volunteer to do it. I am a good masseuse, or so I am told by those like Mami who have been given the gift of a massage by Doris the Healing Hands.

As the last curtain drops, I take a deep breath. I feel light on my feet, like I can fly across the stage. I know I have made it through the hardest time of my life, a year of learning how to find my own way. I have flown against the wind and only lost a few tail feathers. Viva, Doris!

Epilogue

The nestling down is replaced by the juvenile plumage . . .
The juvenile plumage is usually defined as "the first set of true
feathers."

Mami had the surgery, got the pacemaker, and is recovering slowly. But sometimes when we talk on the telephone, she sounds weak. She still sings, she says. In fact, the professor is scheduling a special program at Christmas, so she and I can sing some of the classical Puerto Rican Christmas carols and old romantic boleros together in December. Her Christmas gift to me will be a round-trip ticket to La Isla del Encanto.

"I know it's a long way off," Mami says, "but the early bird . . ."

"Gets the worm!" we both say together, laughing. She admits Abuela's sayings are hard to get out of your head, but she thinks that it's not always a bad thing to have something you can say on any given occasion at the tip of your tongue. "Saves energy," she says.

"And something to say at every *nonoccasion*, too," I add.

Listening to her make plans, I remember a special ritual we had when I was little. Even if it was late, Mami would come into my room and bend over so she could kiss my face very lightly in case I was already asleep.

If I was awake, I would ask her to sing for me. I don't remember ever hearing the end of her songs. I'd be drifting off toward a dream triggered by the song's lyrics, of blue oceans, palm trees, and mountains of emerald green. She always sang when I asked her to, even when she must have been tired. Occasionally, she'd bring me little souvenirs from the places where she'd performed, and I'd get a story to go along with the gift. I see now that these were part of her dream of flying. I still have most of the things she gave me in the same box where I keep Martha's gifts. These pieces of my mother's life are important to me, because, like the scraps of paper and bits of ribbon Martha carried home in her beak, they are messages from the world, reminding me that there is still a lot I have yet to see for myself; and like Doña Iris's people-reading books, the things Mami brought home are my clues to her mind, her heart, and her dreams.

Doña Iris died peacefully. She looked like she was in a deep sleep on her lawn chair. I found her there one morning when I went to feed the birds. I was surprised to see her there. Lately she had been going up on the roof less often because she had trouble making it up the stairs. I guess she wanted to make her final journey in the presence of the birds. The people in our building had been taking turns bringing her food and checking on her. I went once to return her books.

"Claribel," she said, mistaking me for Mami. "That little girl of yours has a gift."

"Doña Iris," I said, sitting on the edge of her bed, "I brought you your books back. The book of dreams and the one on reading people's faces. I learned a lot from them."

"I'm going back to Borinquen," Doña Iris said, calling the island by its original Indian name, as if she had not heard me. "As soon as I find somebody to take care of Juan Pablo's birds, I'm going."

"Doña Iris, I'll take care of the birds. You know I will."

I sang at her funeral.

I sang by myself as they were lowering her into the ground. I made sure I stood straight with my shoulders back and my head raised, arms by my side. Just like the book on body language says self-assured people usually stand. Just like Mami. I sang the song Doña Iris loved best, our island's national anthem, "La Borinqueña."

> *La tierra de Borinquen*
> *donde he nacido yo,*
> *es un jardín florido*
> *de mágico primor.*

Then Papi and Margarita accompanied me with guitar and guiro in a children's song called "Una Paloma Blanca," the white dove.

> *Una paloma blanca*
> *como la nieve*
> *me ha picado en el pecho*

Ay, que me duele.

Ay, ay, ay, que me duele.

On the last note, we released Martha and her fledglings from their box, and let them fly away toward the cloudless sky. I believed that Martha would return home, but the others are young. They might just keep heading toward the horizon. Or maybe the compass they are born with will lead them back to the only home they know. Only time will tell.

I went straight to the roof when I got home from the funeral. Martha was just alighting on the ledge. She returned alone. Although her wing has healed, it is still weak—yet she flew back twenty-five miles from the Garden State Memorial Gardens, where Doña Iris was buried. I've read that racing pigeons can travel hundreds of miles in their prime, but Martha is old. I know the flight must have taken its toll on her.

When I pick Martha up to take her to her nest, I see that she has something in her beak. It's a piece of gold ribbon. It could be from a funeral wreath. At least it looks like it, and I let myself believe that it is. It's a good sign. She still has the energy to find bright things to feather her nest. I gently coax her into her loft. Arturo has decorated it like a gilded castle in curlicues of gold and silver stage paint. She stays in her nest longer now. It's as if she is tired of flying long distances. What was her motivation for going away each day in the first place? I think of Mami saying *"¡Si yo tuviera alas!"* so many times as I was growing up. I guess everyone yearns to fly at some point in their lives.

Martha fixes her eyes on me and coos as if trying to tell me something. I feel her wild little heart beating as I hold her in the palms of my hands. I guess birds live with a sort of permanent tachycardia. Maybe this is why they need to fly away and fly back; maybe it helps to calm their restless hearts. Is Martha ready to settle down now, or just taking a break from her travels? I think she'll keep her plans for the future to herself. And I'll have to wait for the answer. But I am beginning to get her message. I think she is telling me: ¡A volar, Doris¡ *Don't be afraid. It is your turn to look for the treasures you can only see from above.* ¡A volar!

ACKNOWLEDGMENTS

First, foremost, and always, my deepest gratitude to Billie Bennett Franchini, my first and last reader, who has given her blessing to many of my writing projects. Many thanks to my original editor, Melanie Kroupa, for her careful attention to each and every word in this book. And *mil gracias* to my *compañeras* who offered their comments and expertise as this book evolved and changed, among them Kathryn Locey, Betty Jean Craige, and Elena Olazagasti-Segovia. As always, I want to thank John Cofer for his constant encouragement of my work. Finally, I want to express my gratitude to Margaret Ferguson, who brought this book to fruition in the final stages of its development, before we sent it out into the world.